KEAN SOO

MARCH
GRAND PRIX

THE RACE AT HAREWOOD

STONE ARCH BOOKS
a capstone imprint

March Grand Prix
published by Stone Arch Books,
a Capstone Imprint
1710 Roe Crest Drive
North Mankato, Minnesota 56003
www.capstonepub.com

Cataloging-in-Publication Data is available on
the Library of Congress website.

ISBN: 978-1-4342-9639-9 (library hardcover)
ISBN: 978-1-4342-9642-9 (paperback)
ISBN: 978-1-4965-0184-4 (eBook)

Summary: March Hare enters into his first
professional race at Harewood Speedway
and comes up against the defending World
Champion, Lyca the Fox, whose skills are
unrivaled. March finds help and inspiration in
the unlikeliest of places — his own family.

Printed in China by Nordica.
0415/CA21500596
042015   008843NORDF15

To Mom and Dad,

*For all the times you drove me around
in the backseat of the car, trying to get
me to fall asleep. And for all the times
I woke up as soon as we got home.*

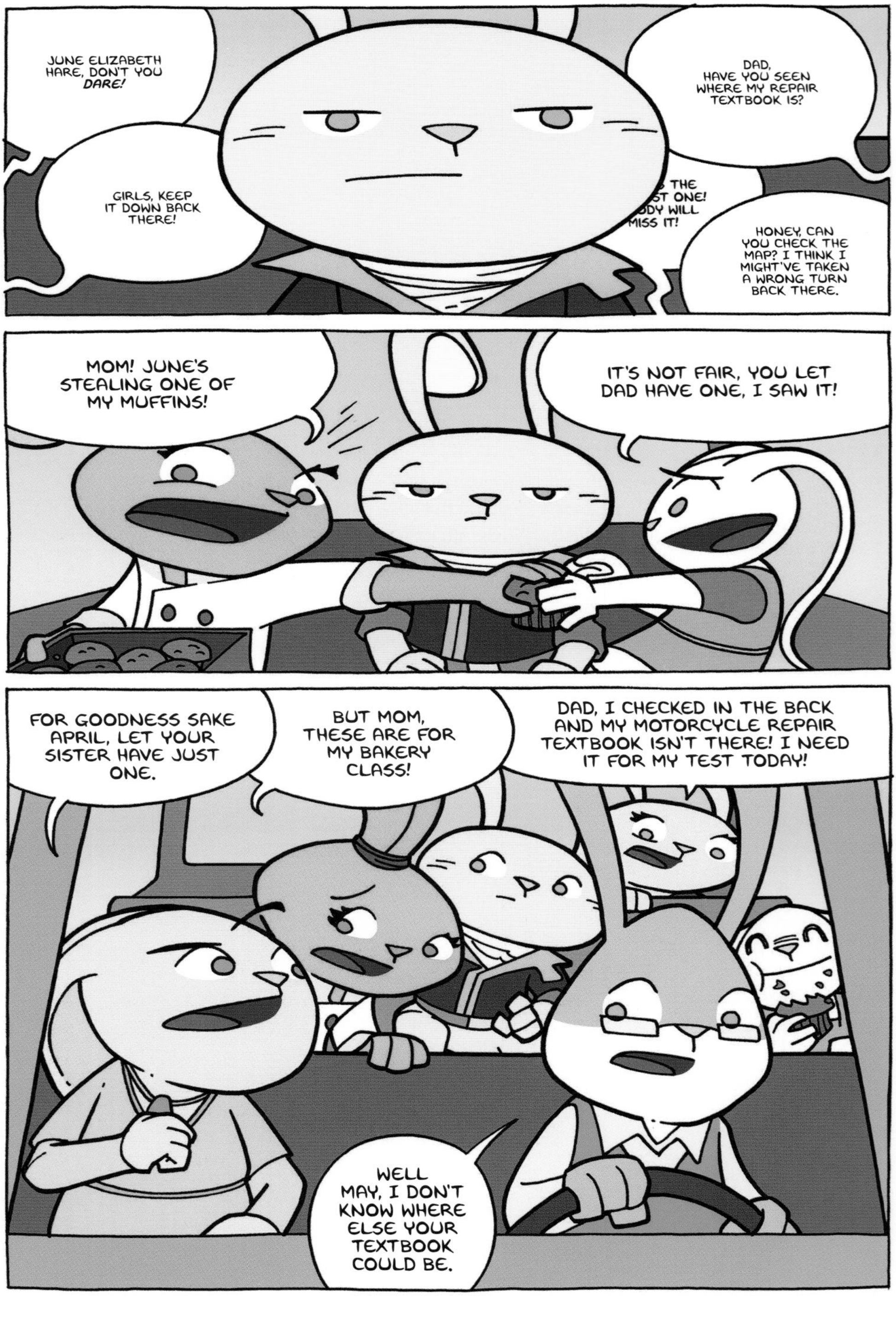
JUNE ELIZABETH HARE, DON'T YOU *DARE!*
GIRLS, KEEP IT DOWN BACK THERE!
DAD, HAVE YOU SEEN WHERE MY REPAIR TEXTBOOK IS?
HONEY, CAN YOU CHECK THE MAP? I THINK I MIGHT'VE TAKEN A WRONG TURN BACK THERE.
MOM! JUNE'S STEALING ONE OF MY MUFFINS!
IT'S NOT FAIR, YOU LET DAD HAVE ONE, I SAW IT!
FOR GOODNESS SAKE APRIL, LET YOUR SISTER HAVE JUST ONE.
BUT MOM, THESE ARE FOR MY BAKERY CLASS!
DAD, I CHECKED IN THE BACK AND MY MOTORCYCLE REPAIR TEXTBOOK ISN'T THERE! I NEED IT FOR MY TEST TODAY!
WELL MAY, I DON'T KNOW WHERE ELSE YOUR TEXTBOOK COULD BE.

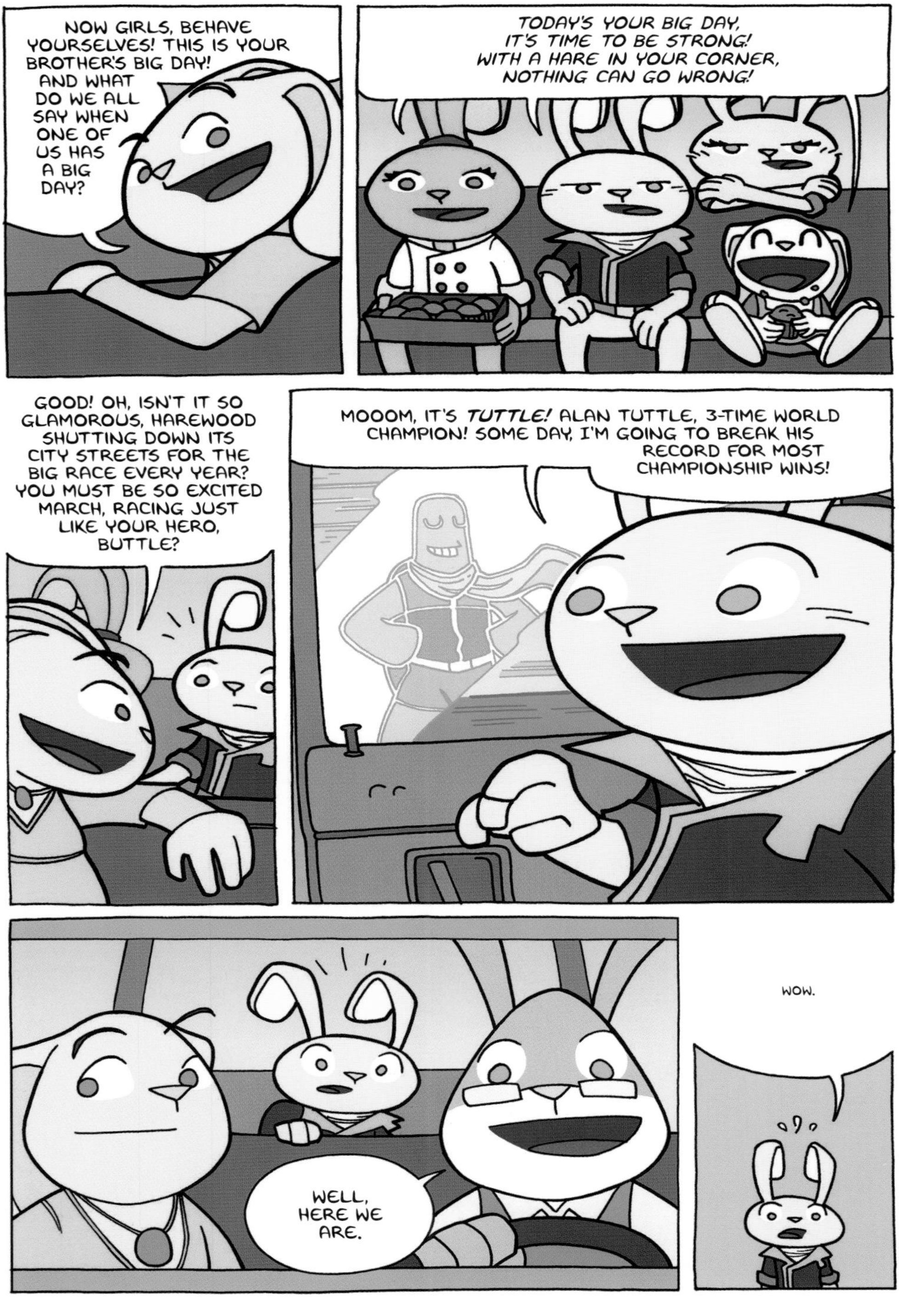
NOW GIRLS, BEHAVE YOURSELVES! THIS IS YOUR BROTHER'S BIG DAY! AND WHAT DO WE ALL SAY WHEN ONE OF US HAS A BIG DAY?
TODAY'S YOUR BIG DAY, IT'S TIME TO BE STRONG! WITH A HARE IN YOUR CORNER, NOTHING CAN GO WRONG!
GOOD! OH, ISN'T IT SO GLAMOROUS, HAREWOOD SHUTTING DOWN ITS CITY STREETS FOR THE BIG RACE EVERY YEAR? YOU MUST BE SO EXCITED MARCH, RACING JUST LIKE YOUR HERO, BUTTLE?
MOOOM, IT'S TUTTLE! ALAN TUTTLE, 3-TIME WORLD CHAMPION! SOME DAY, I'M GOING TO BREAK HIS RECORD FOR MOST CHAMPIONSHIP WINS!
WELL, HERE WE ARE.
WOW.

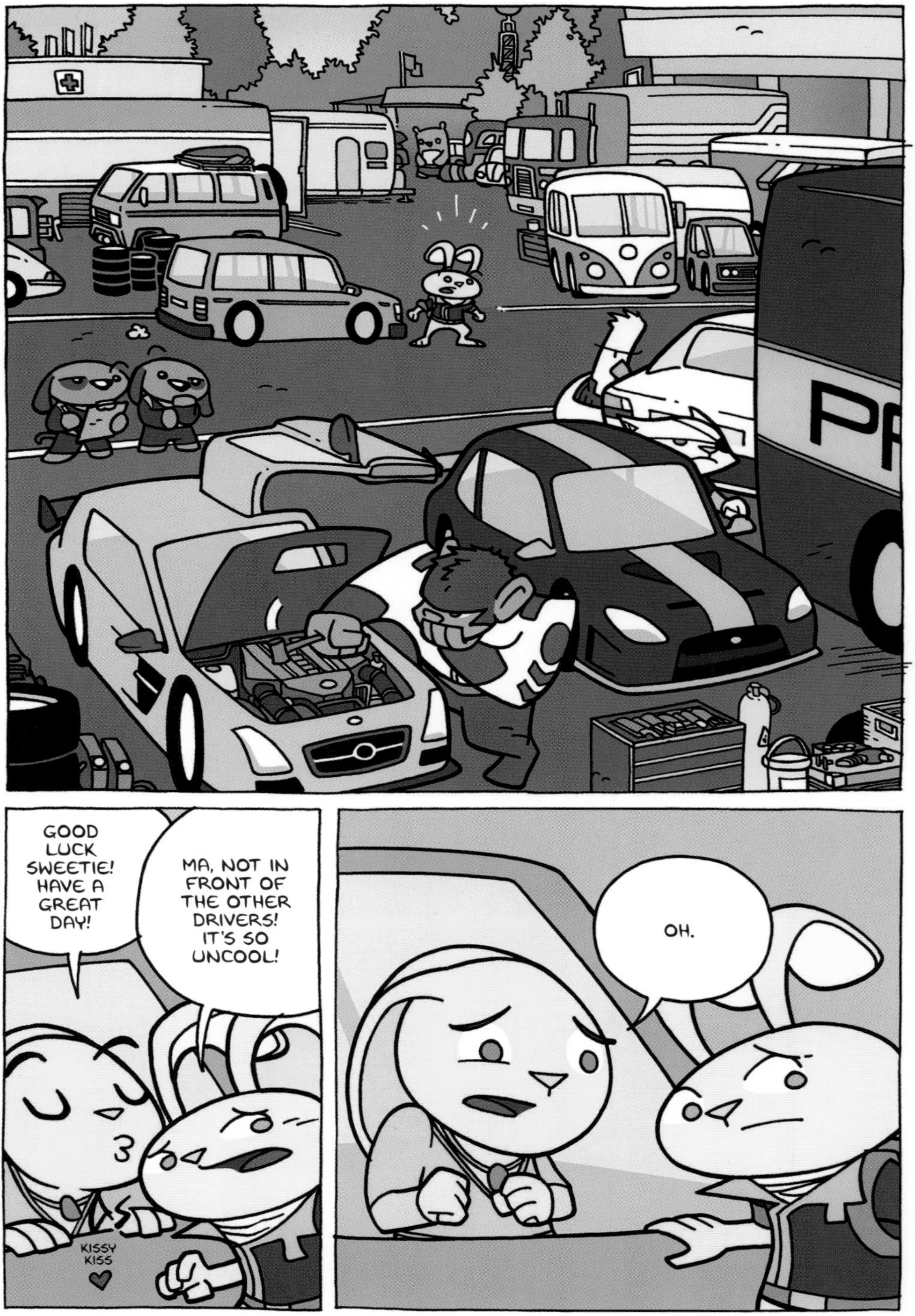
GOOD LUCK SWEETIE! HAVE A GREAT DAY!
MA, NOT IN FRONT OF THE OTHER DRIVERS! IT'S SO UNCOOL!
KISSY KISS
OH.

WELL, WE'RE PROUD OF YOU AND WE'RE NOT GOING TO HIDE IT. WE'RE ALWAYS HERE FOR YOU IF YOU NEED US.

OKAY! HAVE A GREAT DAY! AND REMEMBER:

WE LOVE YOU!

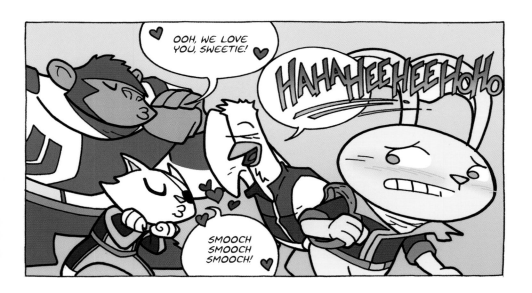

OOH, WE LOVE YOU, SWEETIE!

HAHAHEEHEEHOHO

SMOOCH SMOOCH SMOOCH!

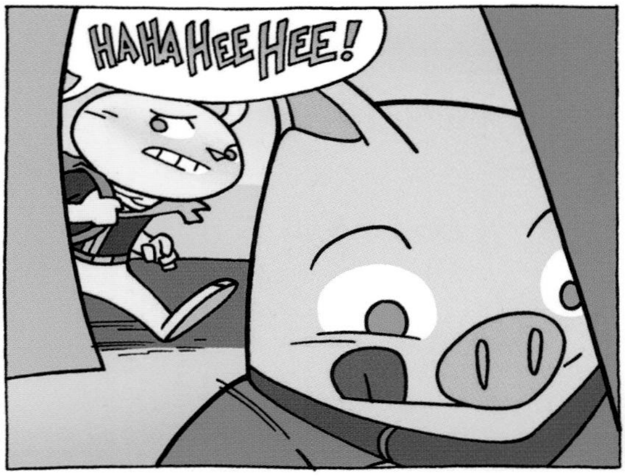
HAHAHEEHEE!

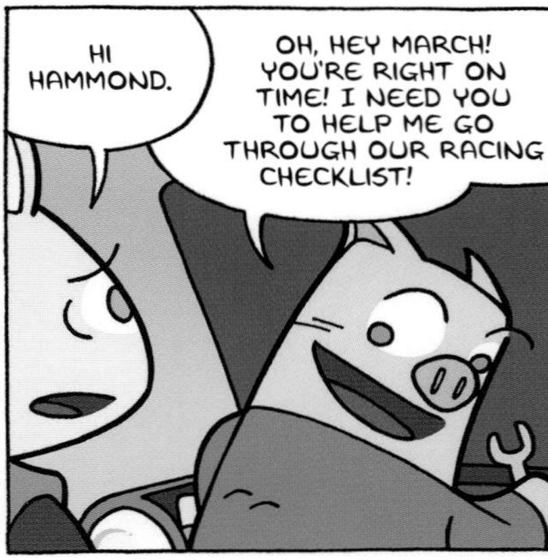
HI HAMMOND.
OH, HEY MARCH! YOU'RE RIGHT ON TIME! I NEED YOU TO HELP ME GO THROUGH OUR RACING CHECKLIST!

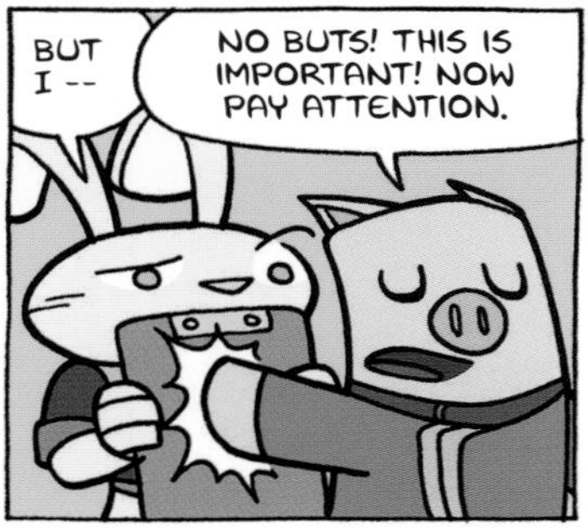
BUT I --
NO BUTS! THIS IS IMPORTANT! NOW PAY ATTENTION.

GT-R Superturbo

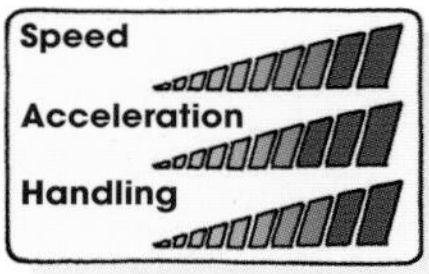
Speed
Acceleration
Handling

Class: Subcompact 3-door racing hatchback
Layout: FF layout (Front-engine, Front-wheel-drive)

Engine: 1.4-Liter, 16-valve twin charged inline four-cylinder
Power: 200 hp
Torque: 220 lb/ft @3000 rpm

Transmission: 5-speed manual

Curb weight: 1,488 lb

Top speed: 125 mph
0-60 mph: 6.5 seconds

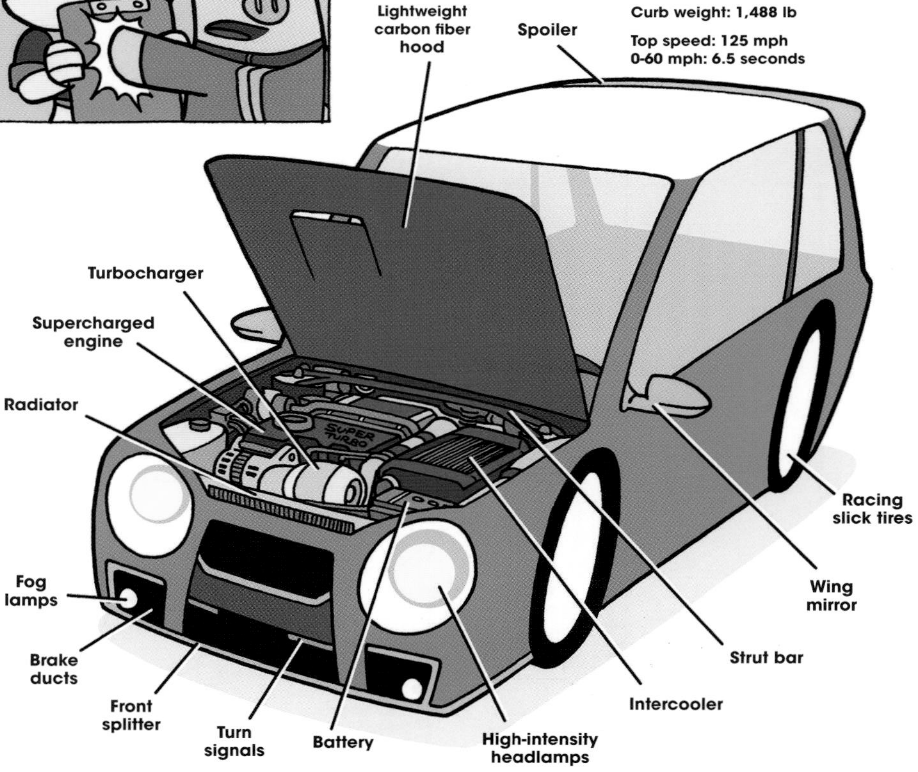
Lightweight carbon fiber hood
Spoiler
Turbocharger
Supercharged engine
Radiator
SUPER TURBO
Racing slick tires
Wing mirror
Fog lamps
Brake ducts
Strut bar
Intercooler
Front splitter
Turn signals
Battery
High-intensity headlamps

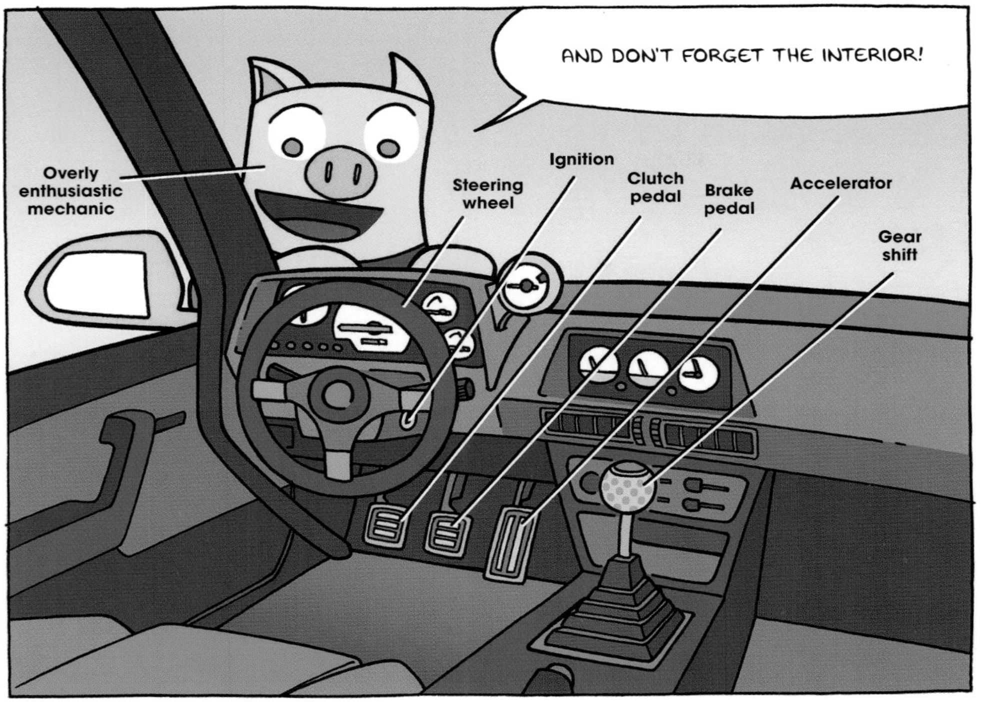
AND DON'T FORGET THE INTERIOR!
Overly enthusiastic mechanic
Steering wheel
Ignition
Clutch pedal
Brake pedal
Accelerator
Gear shift

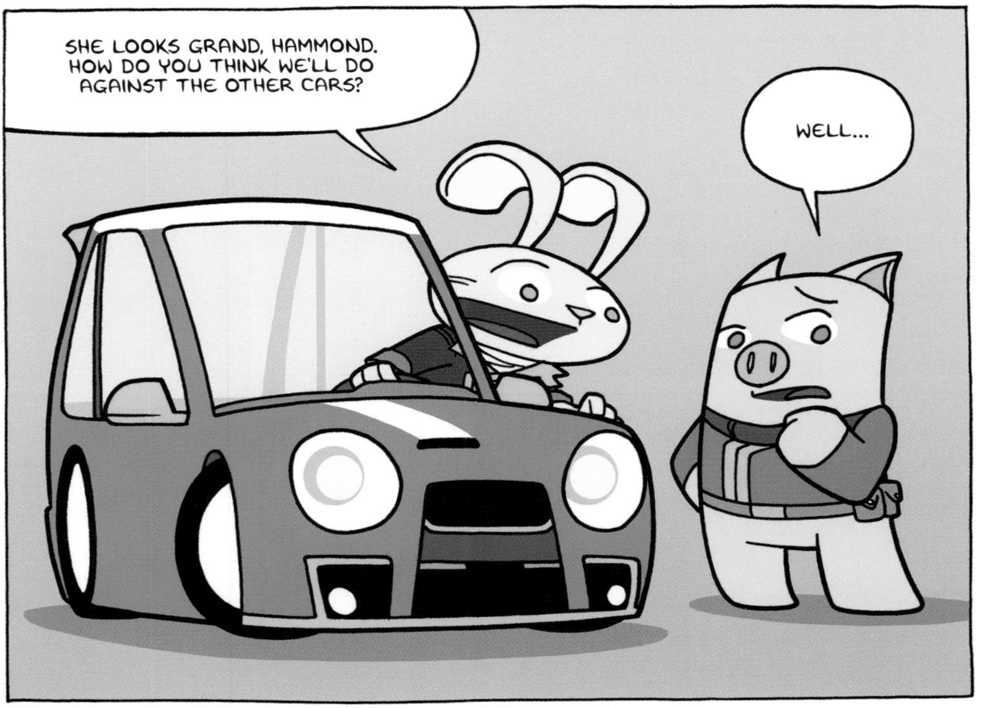
SHE LOOKS GRAND, HAMMOND. HOW DO YOU THINK WE'LL DO AGAINST THE OTHER CARS?
WELL...

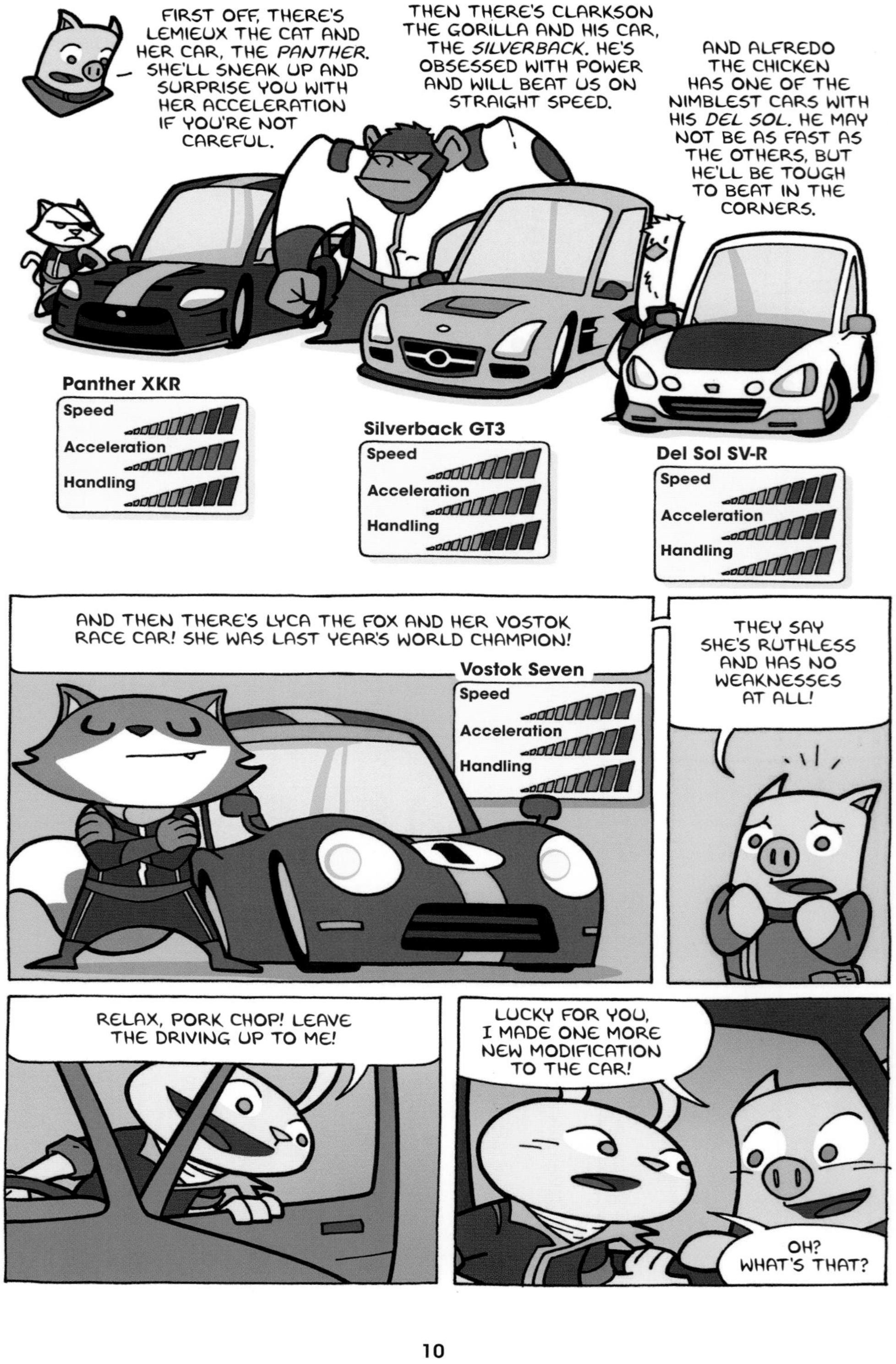
FIRST OFF, THERE'S LEMIEUX THE CAT AND HER CAR, THE PANTHER. SHE'LL SNEAK UP AND SURPRISE YOU WITH HER ACCELERATION IF YOU'RE NOT CAREFUL.
THEN THERE'S CLARKSON THE GORILLA AND HIS CAR, THE SILVERBACK. HE'S OBSESSED WITH POWER AND WILL BEAT US ON STRAIGHT SPEED.
AND ALFREDO THE CHICKEN HAS ONE OF THE NIMBLEST CARS WITH HIS DEL SOL. HE MAY NOT BE AS FAST AS THE OTHERS, BUT HE'LL BE TOUGH TO BEAT IN THE CORNERS.
Panther XKR
Speed
Acceleration
Handling
Silverback GT3
Speed
Acceleration
Handling
Del Sol SV-R
Speed
Acceleration
Handling
AND THEN THERE'S LYCA THE FOX AND HER VOSTOK RACE CAR! SHE WAS LAST YEAR'S WORLD CHAMPION!
Vostok Seven
Speed
Acceleration
Handling
THEY SAY SHE'S RUTHLESS AND HAS NO WEAKNESSES AT ALL!
RELAX, PORK CHOP! LEAVE THE DRIVING UP TO ME!
LUCKY FOR YOU, I MADE ONE MORE NEW MODIFICATION TO THE CAR!
OH? WHAT'S THAT?

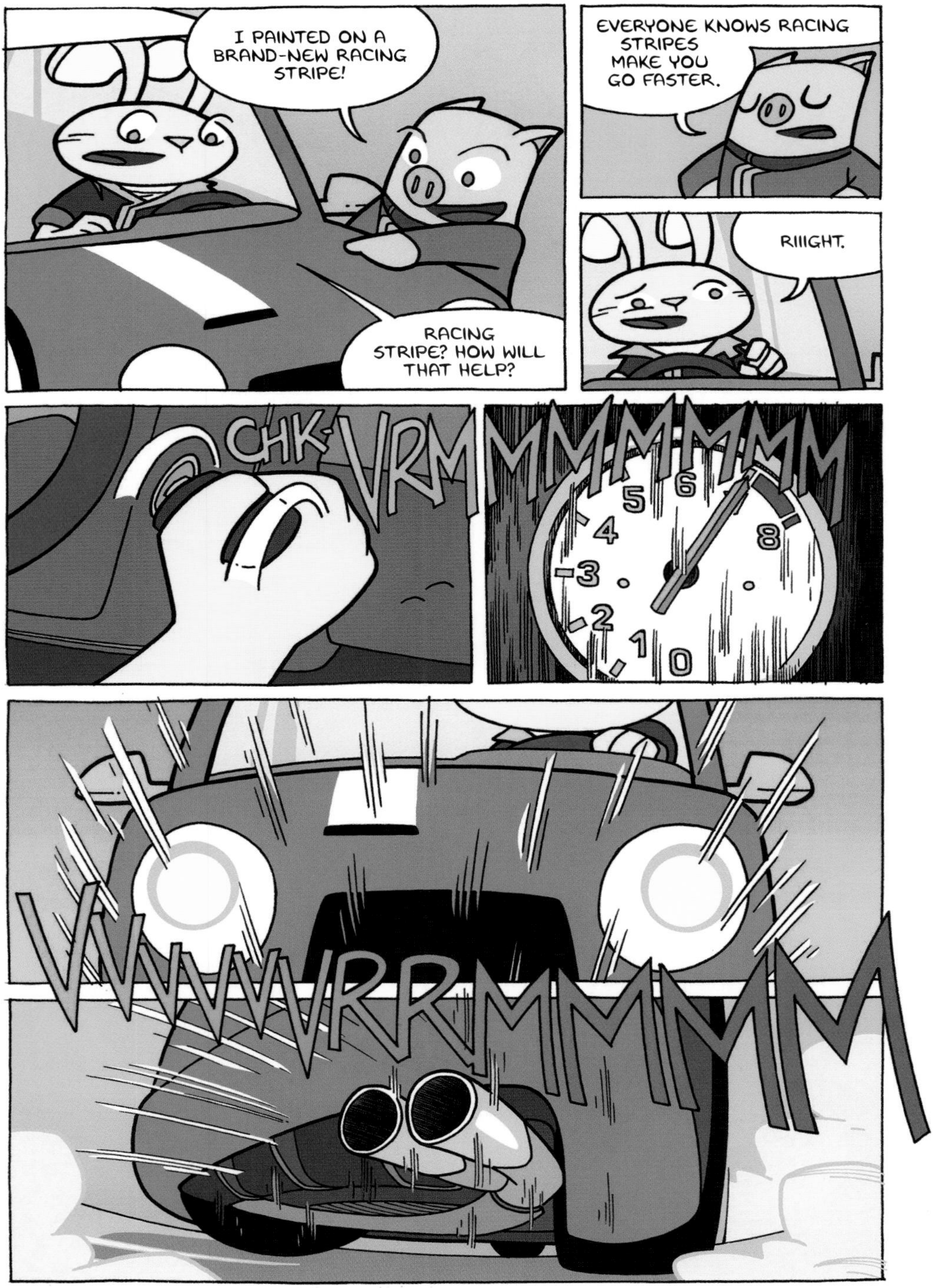
I PAINTED ON A BRAND-NEW RACING STRIPE!
RACING STRIPE? HOW WILL THAT HELP?
EVERYONE KNOWS RACING STRIPES MAKE YOU GO FASTER.
RIIIGHT.
CHK-
VRMMMMMMMM
VVVVVVRRMMMMMMM

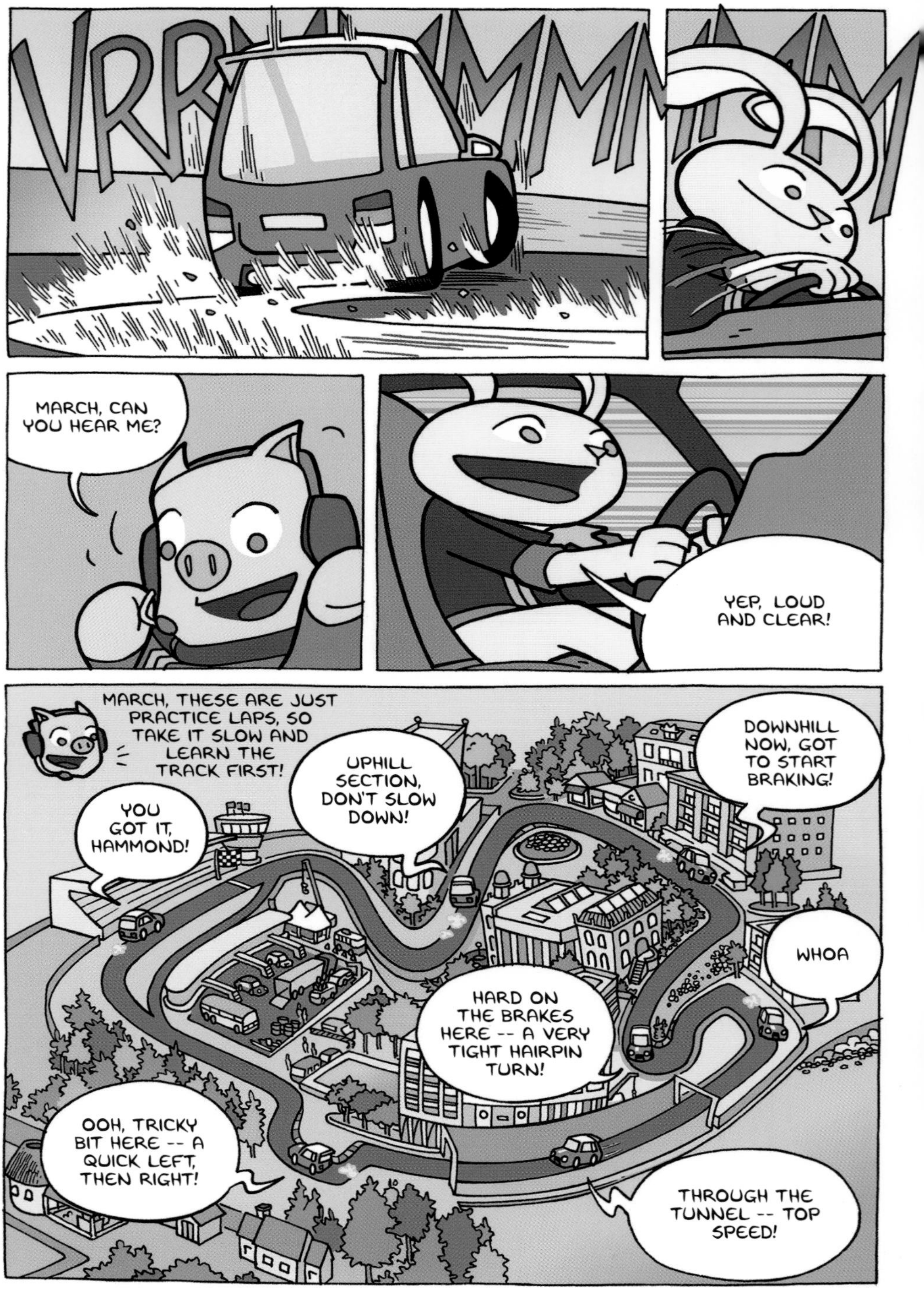
VRRMMMMMMMMM
MARCH, CAN YOU HEAR ME?
YEP, LOUD AND CLEAR!
MARCH, THESE ARE JUST PRACTICE LAPS, SO TAKE IT SLOW AND LEARN THE TRACK FIRST!
YOU GOT IT, HAMMOND!
UPHILL SECTION, DON'T SLOW DOWN!
DOWNHILL NOW, GOT TO START BRAKING!
WHOA
HARD ON THE BRAKES HERE -- A VERY TIGHT HAIRPIN TURN!
OOH, TRICKY BIT HERE -- A QUICK LEFT, THEN RIGHT!
THROUGH THE TUNNEL -- TOP SPEED!

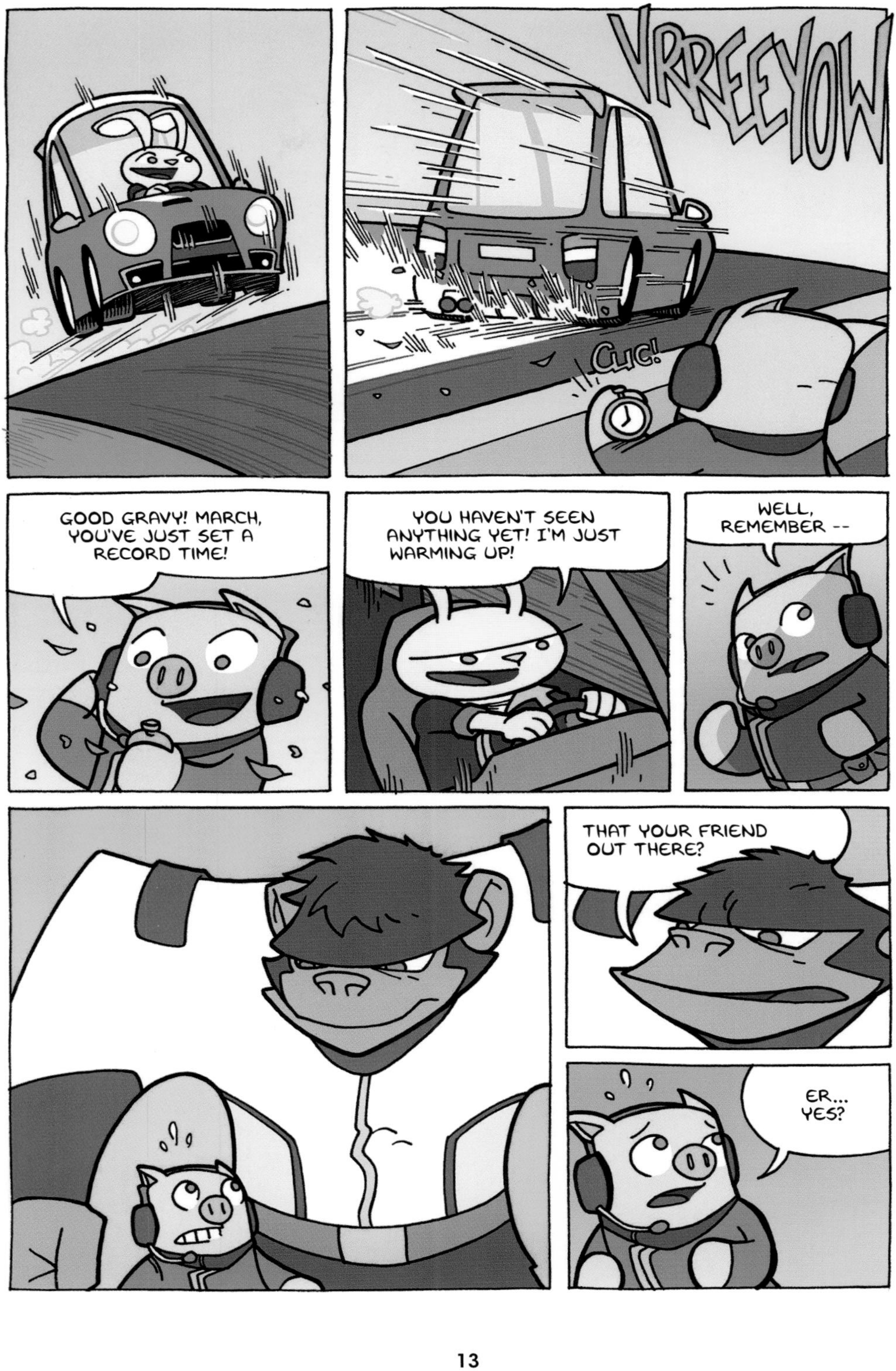
VRREEYOW
CLIC!
GOOD GRAVY! MARCH, YOU'VE JUST SET A RECORD TIME!
YOU HAVEN'T SEEN ANYTHING YET! I'M JUST WARMING UP!
WELL, REMEMBER --
THAT YOUR FRIEND OUT THERE?
ER... YES?

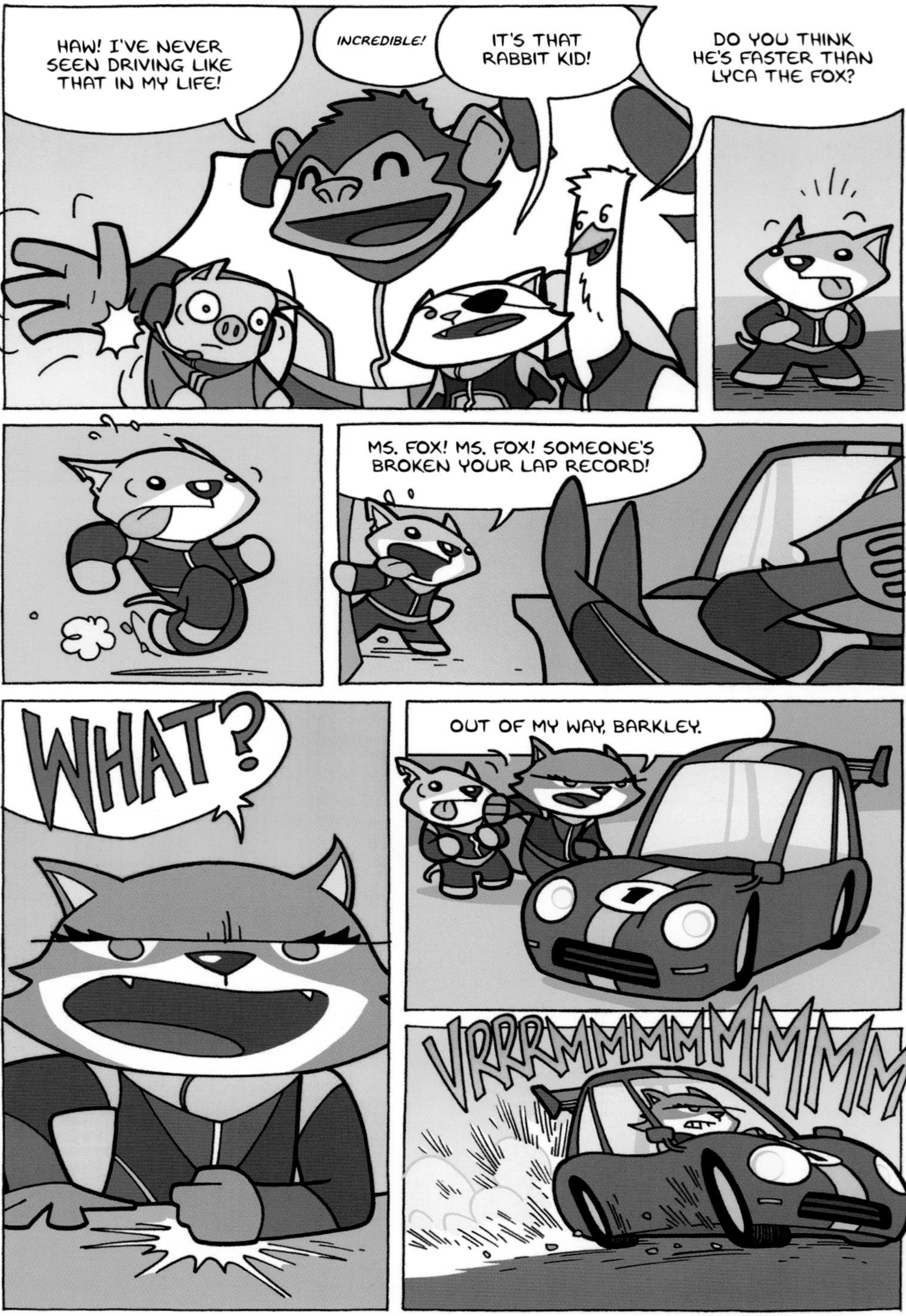
HAW! I'VE NEVER SEEN DRIVING LIKE THAT IN MY LIFE!
INCREDIBLE!
IT'S THAT RABBIT KID!
DO YOU THINK HE'S FASTER THAN LYCA THE FOX?
MS. FOX! MS. FOX! SOMEONE'S BROKEN YOUR LAP RECORD!
WHAT?
OUT OF MY WAY, BARKLEY.
VRRRMMMMMMMMMM

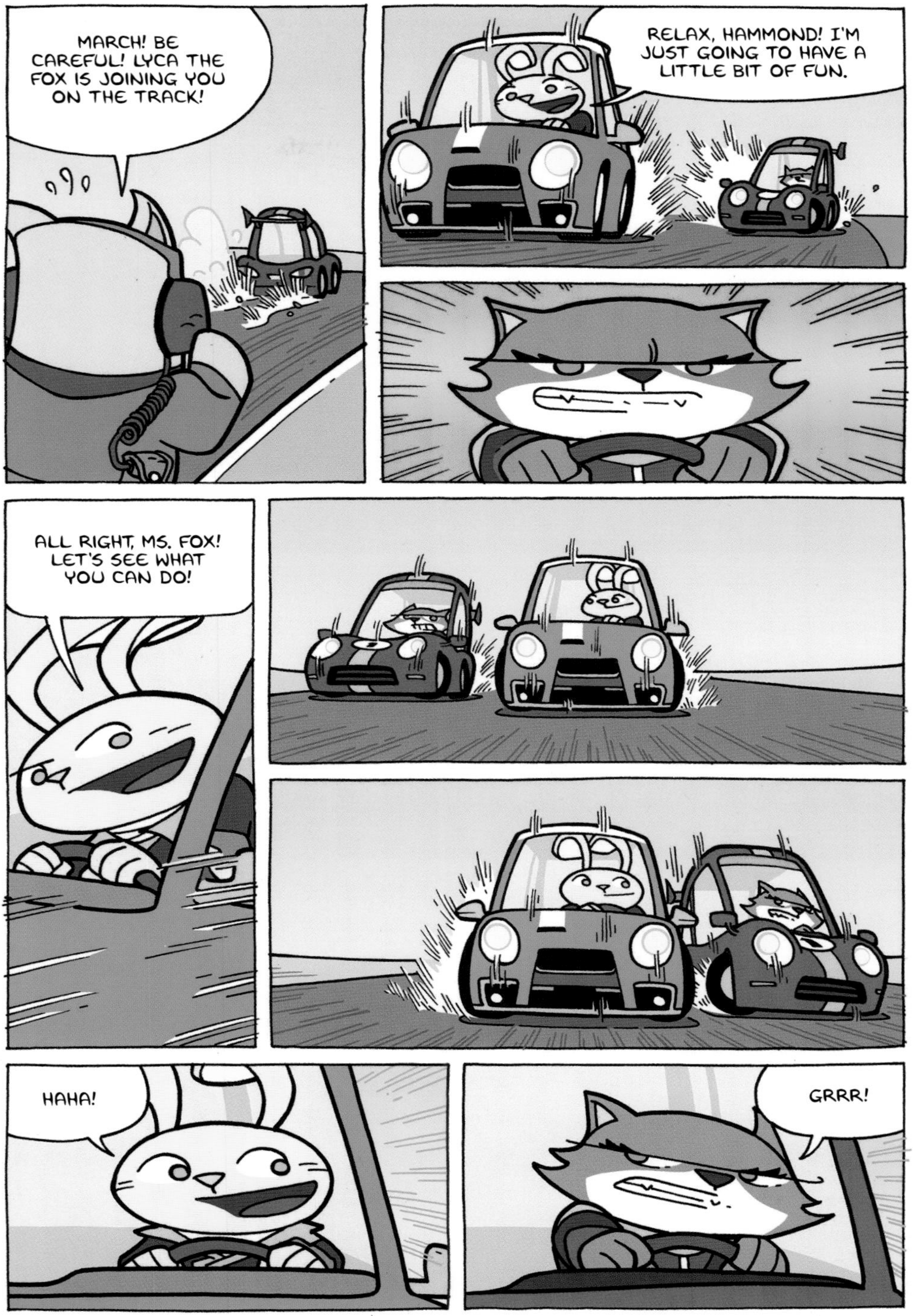
MARCH! BE CAREFUL! LYCA THE FOX IS JOINING YOU ON THE TRACK!
RELAX, HAMMOND! I'M JUST GOING TO HAVE A LITTLE BIT OF FUN.
ALL RIGHT, MS. FOX! LET'S SEE WHAT YOU CAN DO!
HAHA!
GRRR!

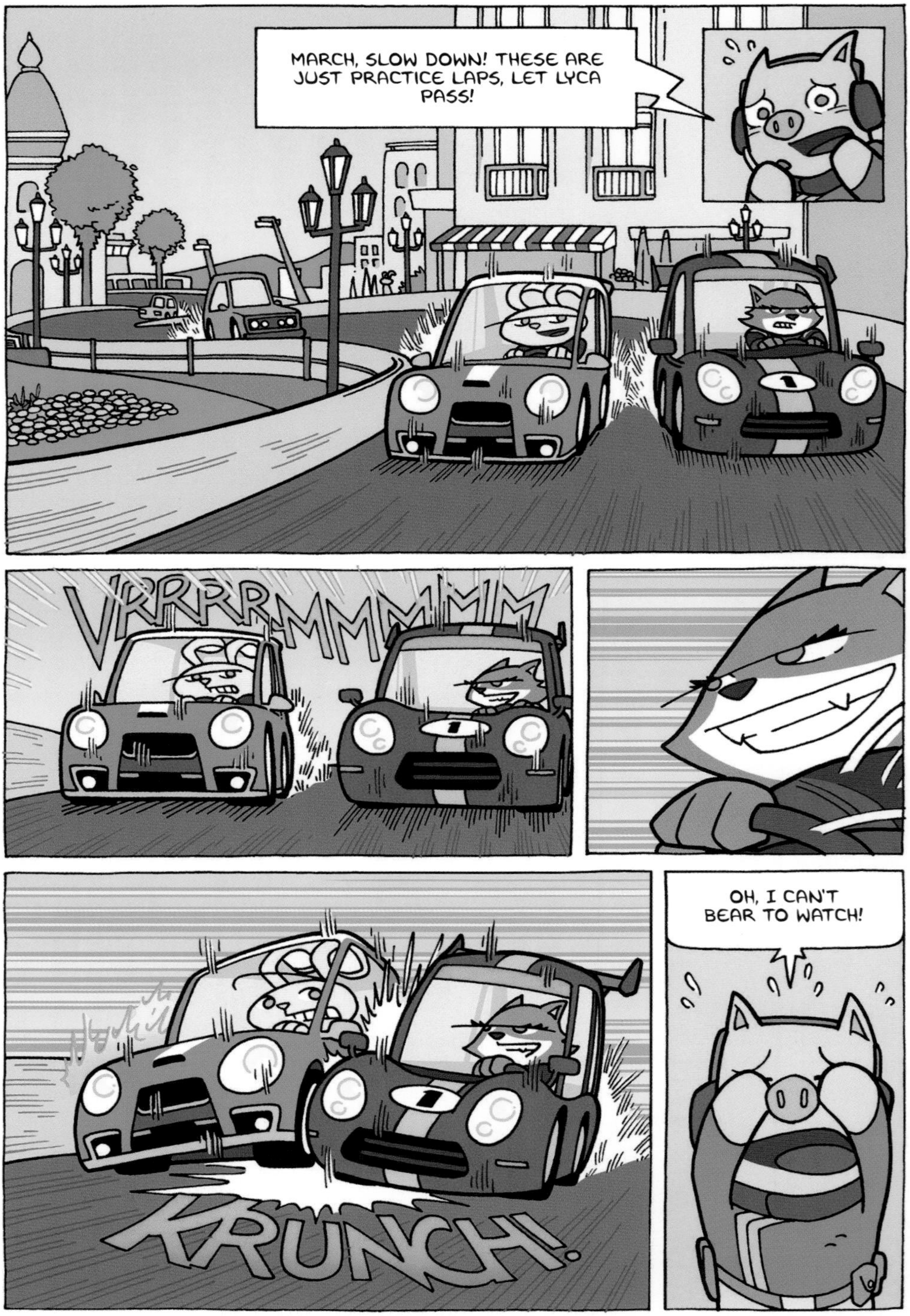
MARCH, SLOW DOWN! THESE ARE JUST PRACTICE LAPS, LET LYCA PASS!
VRRRRMMMMM
KRUNCH!
OH, I CAN'T BEAR TO WATCH!

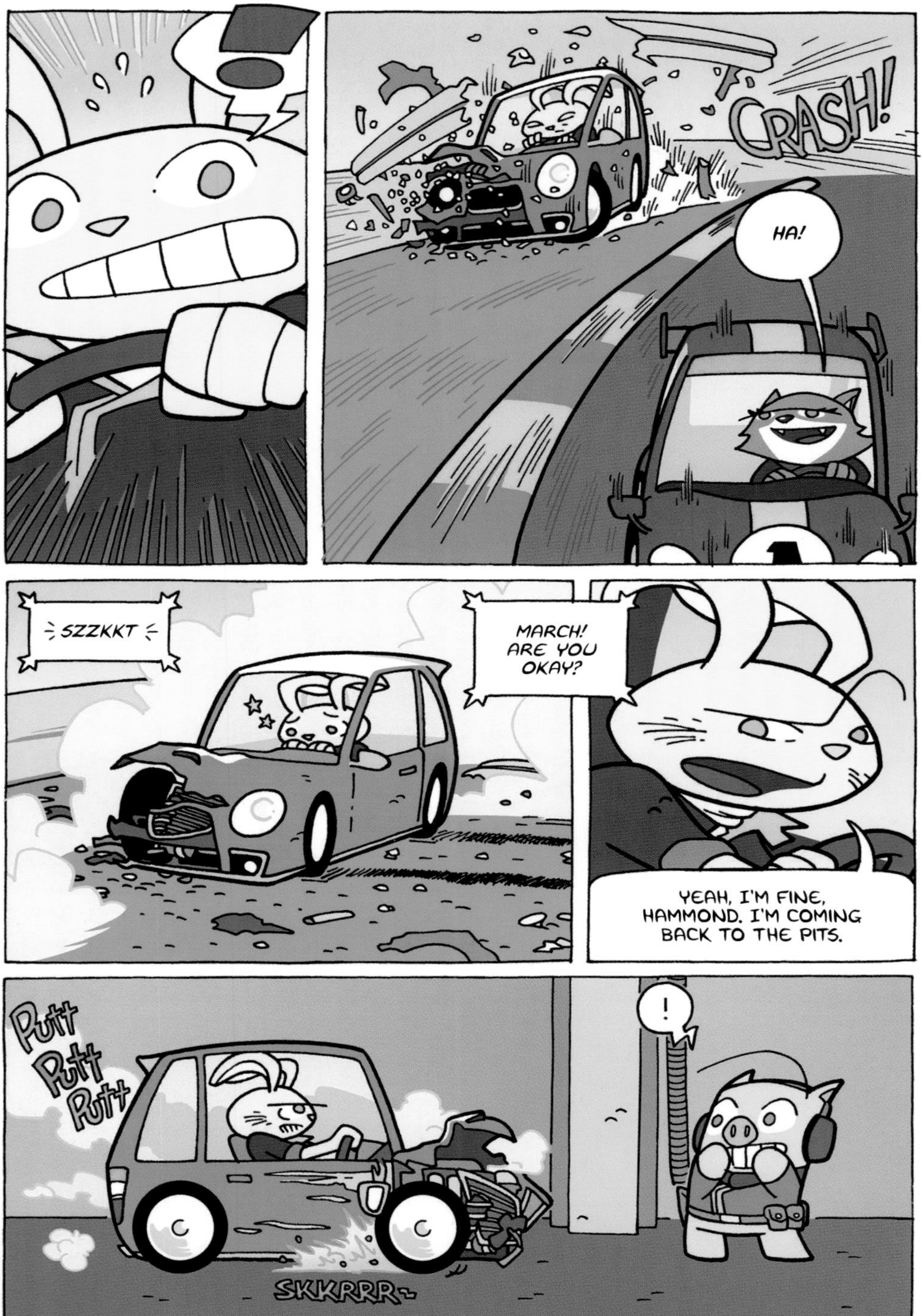
CRASH!
HA!
SZZKKT
MARCH! ARE YOU OKAY?
YEAH, I'M FINE, HAMMOND. I'M COMING BACK TO THE PITS.
Putt Putt Putt
!
SKKRRR

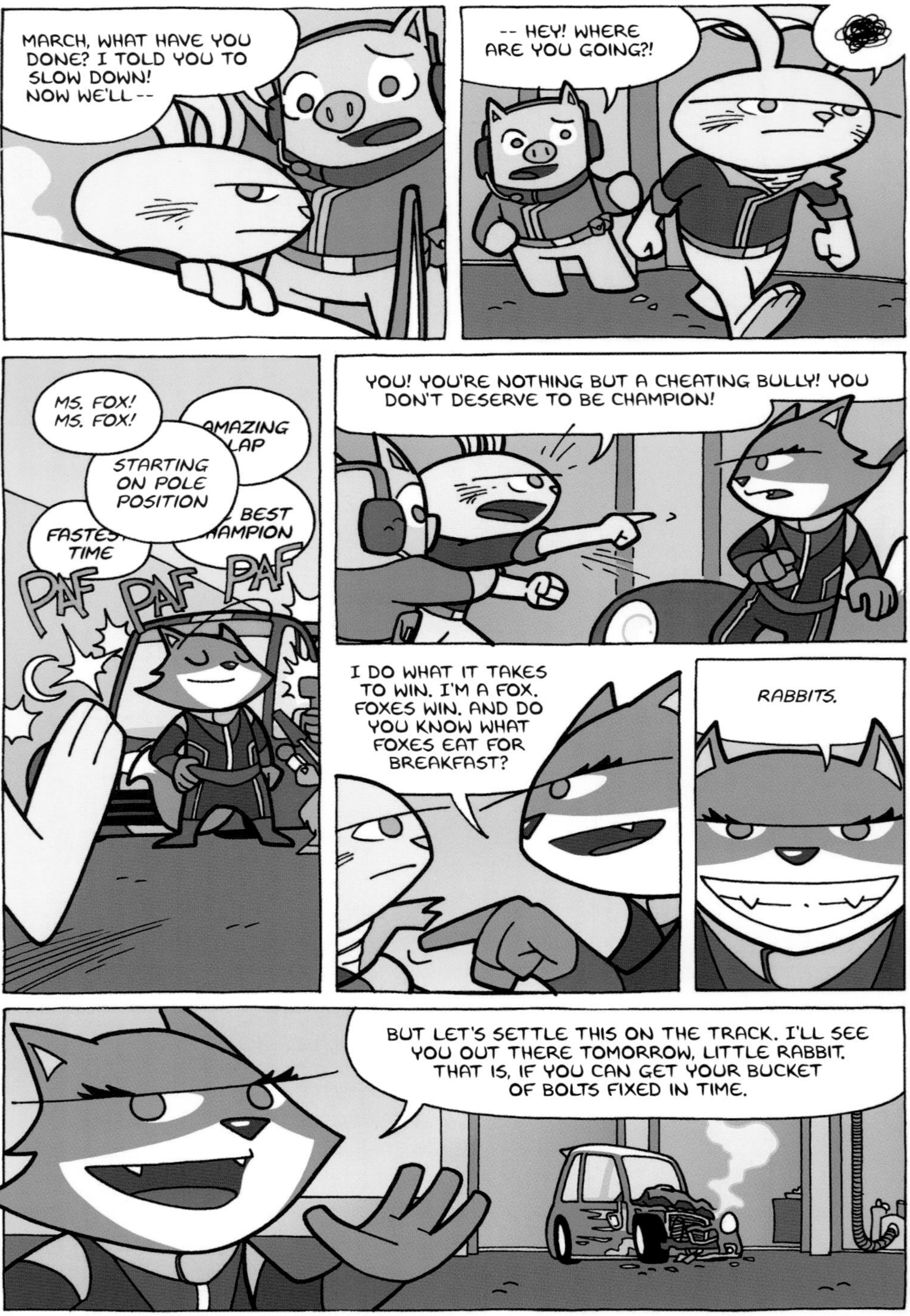

MARCH, WHAT HAVE YOU DONE? I TOLD YOU TO SLOW DOWN! NOW WE'LL--
-- HEY! WHERE ARE YOU GOING?!
MS. FOX! MS. FOX!
AMAZING LAP
STARTING ON POLE POSITION
BEST CHAMPION
FASTEST TIME
PAF PAF PAF
YOU! YOU'RE NOTHING BUT A CHEATING BULLY! YOU DON'T DESERVE TO BE CHAMPION!
I DO WHAT IT TAKES TO WIN. I'M A FOX. FOXES WIN. AND DO YOU KNOW WHAT FOXES EAT FOR BREAKFAST?
RABBITS.
BUT LET'S SETTLE THIS ON THE TRACK. I'LL SEE YOU OUT THERE TOMORROW, LITTLE RABBIT. THAT IS, IF YOU CAN GET YOUR BUCKET OF BOLTS FIXED IN TIME.

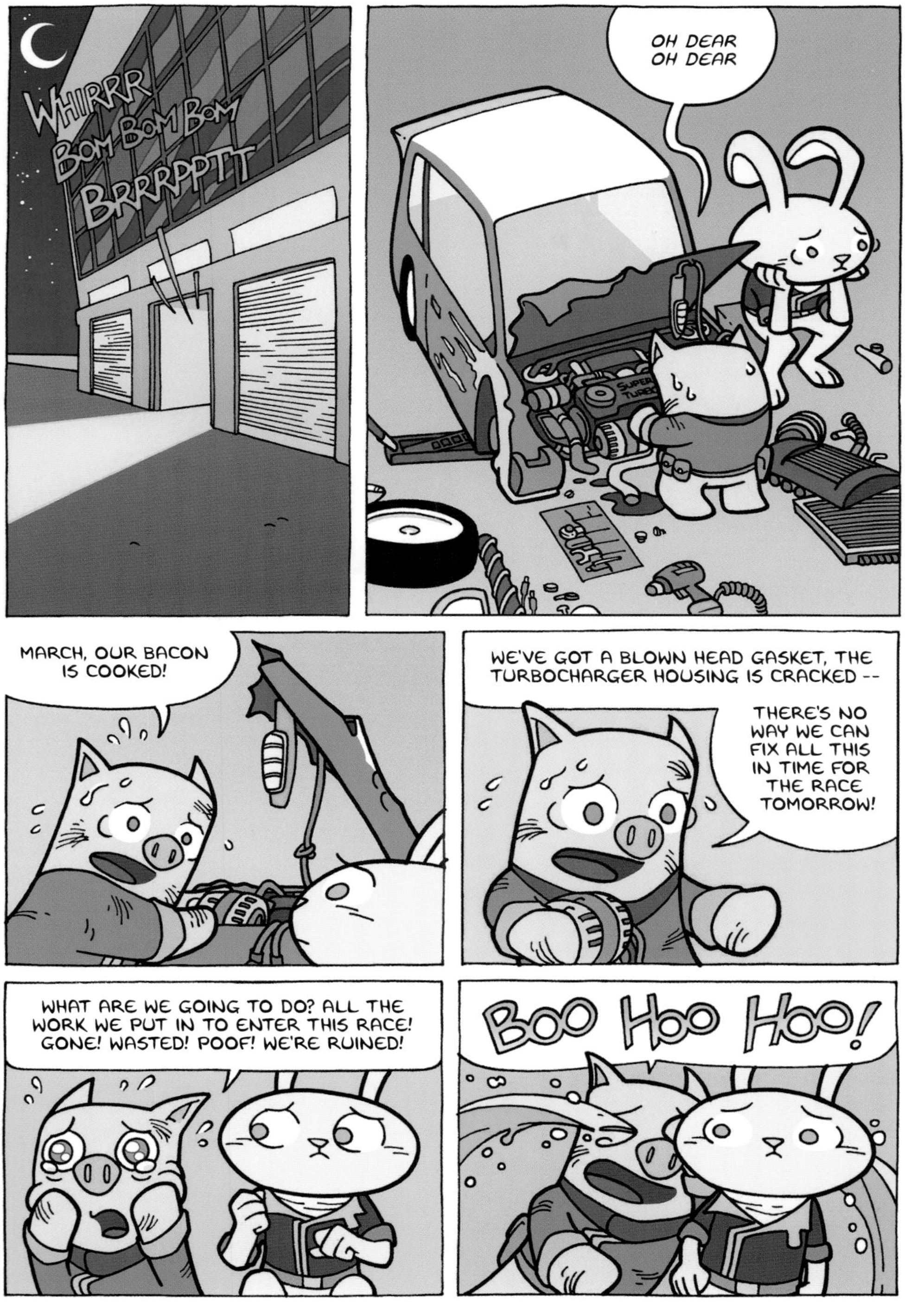
WHIRRR
BOM BOM BOM
BRRRPPTT
OH DEAR
OH DEAR
SUPER TURBO
MARCH, OUR BACON IS COOKED!
WE'VE GOT A BLOWN HEAD GASKET, THE TURBOCHARGER HOUSING IS CRACKED --
THERE'S NO WAY WE CAN FIX ALL THIS IN TIME FOR THE RACE TOMORROW!
WHAT ARE WE GOING TO DO? ALL THE WORK WE PUT IN TO ENTER THIS RACE! GONE! WASTED! POOF! WE'RE RUINED!
BOO HOO HOO!

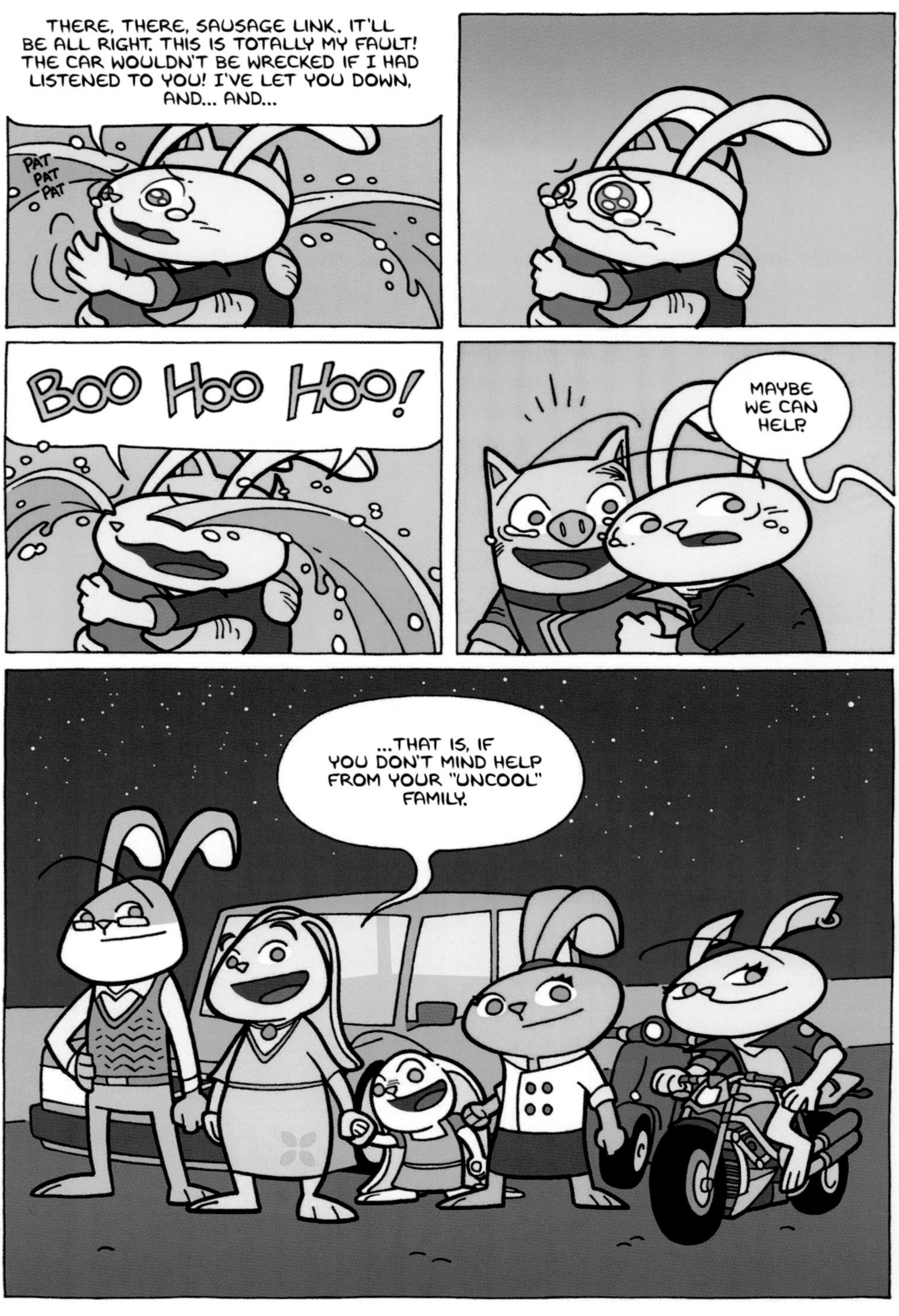
THERE, THERE, SAUSAGE LINK. IT'LL BE ALL RIGHT. THIS IS TOTALLY MY FAULT! THE CAR WOULDN'T BE WRECKED IF I HAD LISTENED TO YOU! I'VE LET YOU DOWN, AND... AND...
PAT PAT PAT
BOO HOO HOO!
MAYBE WE CAN HELP.
...THAT IS, IF YOU DON'T MIND HELP FROM YOUR "UNCOOL" FAMILY.

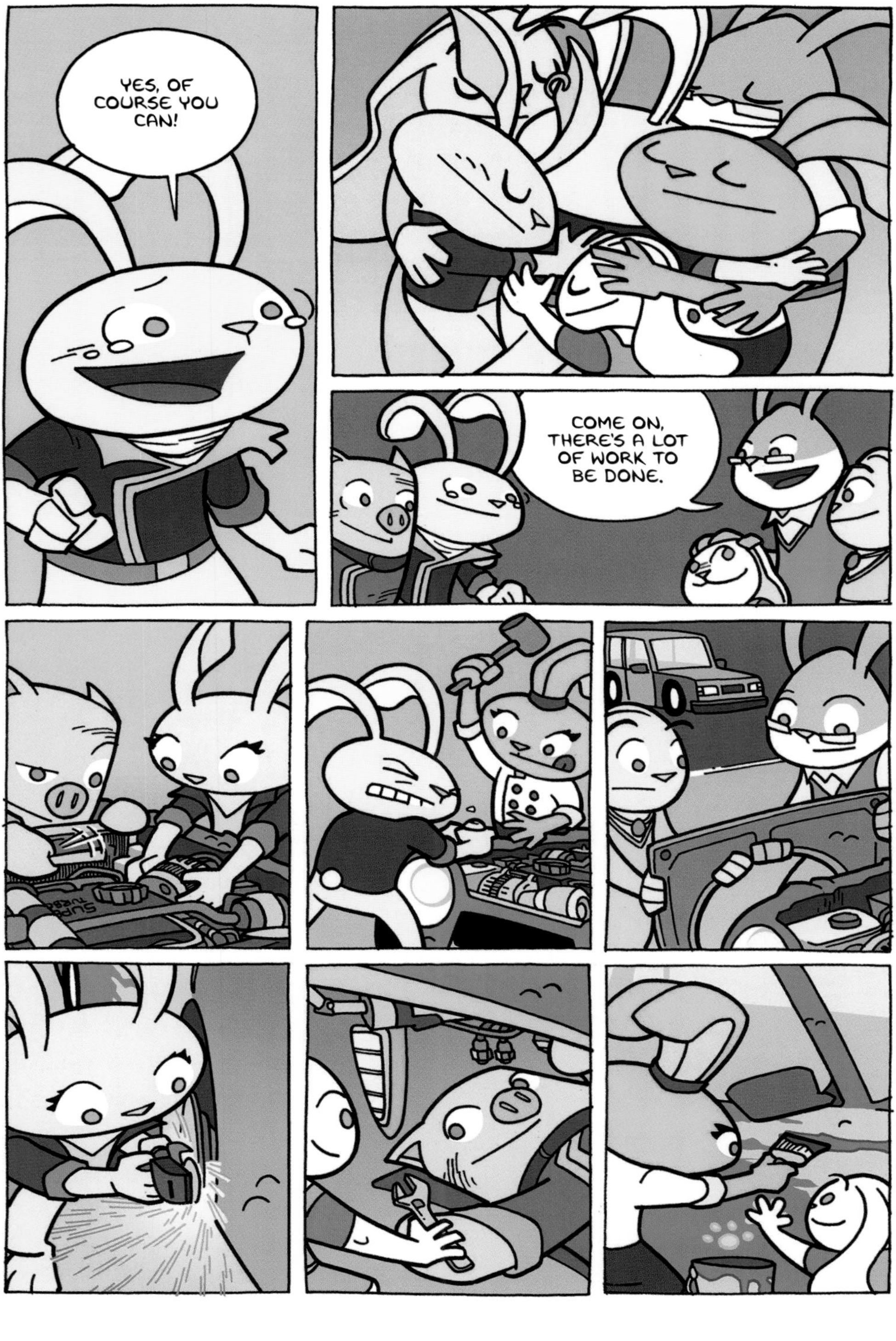
YES, OF COURSE YOU CAN!
COME ON, THERE'S A LOT OF WORK TO BE DONE.

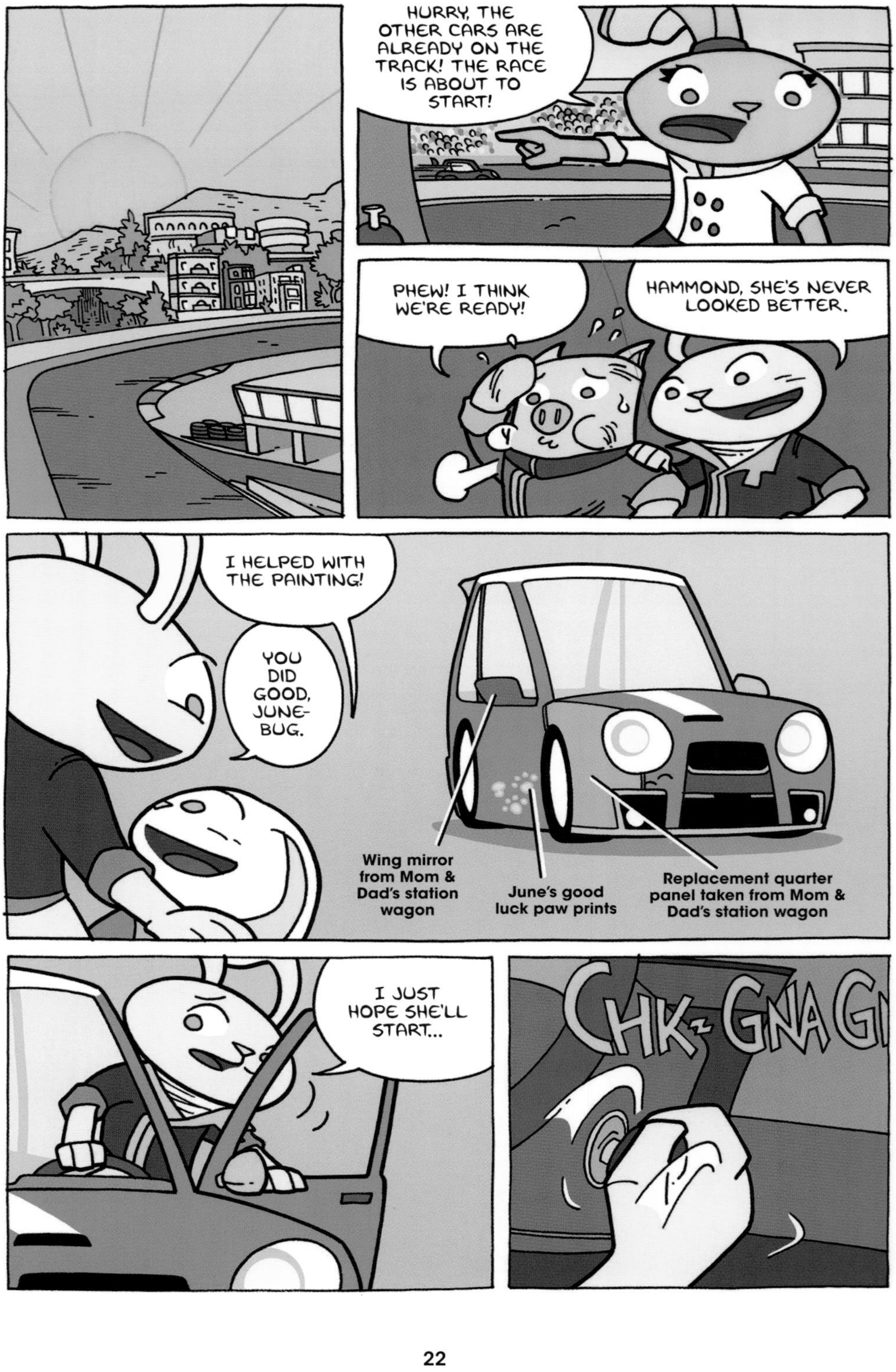
HURRY, THE OTHER CARS ARE ALREADY ON THE TRACK! THE RACE IS ABOUT TO START!
PHEW! I THINK WE'RE READY!
HAMMOND, SHE'S NEVER LOOKED BETTER.
I HELPED WITH THE PAINTING!
YOU DID GOOD, JUNE-BUG.
Wing mirror from Mom & Dad's station wagon
June's good luck paw prints
Replacement quarter panel taken from Mom & Dad's station wagon
I JUST HOPE SHE'LL START...
CHK-GNAGN

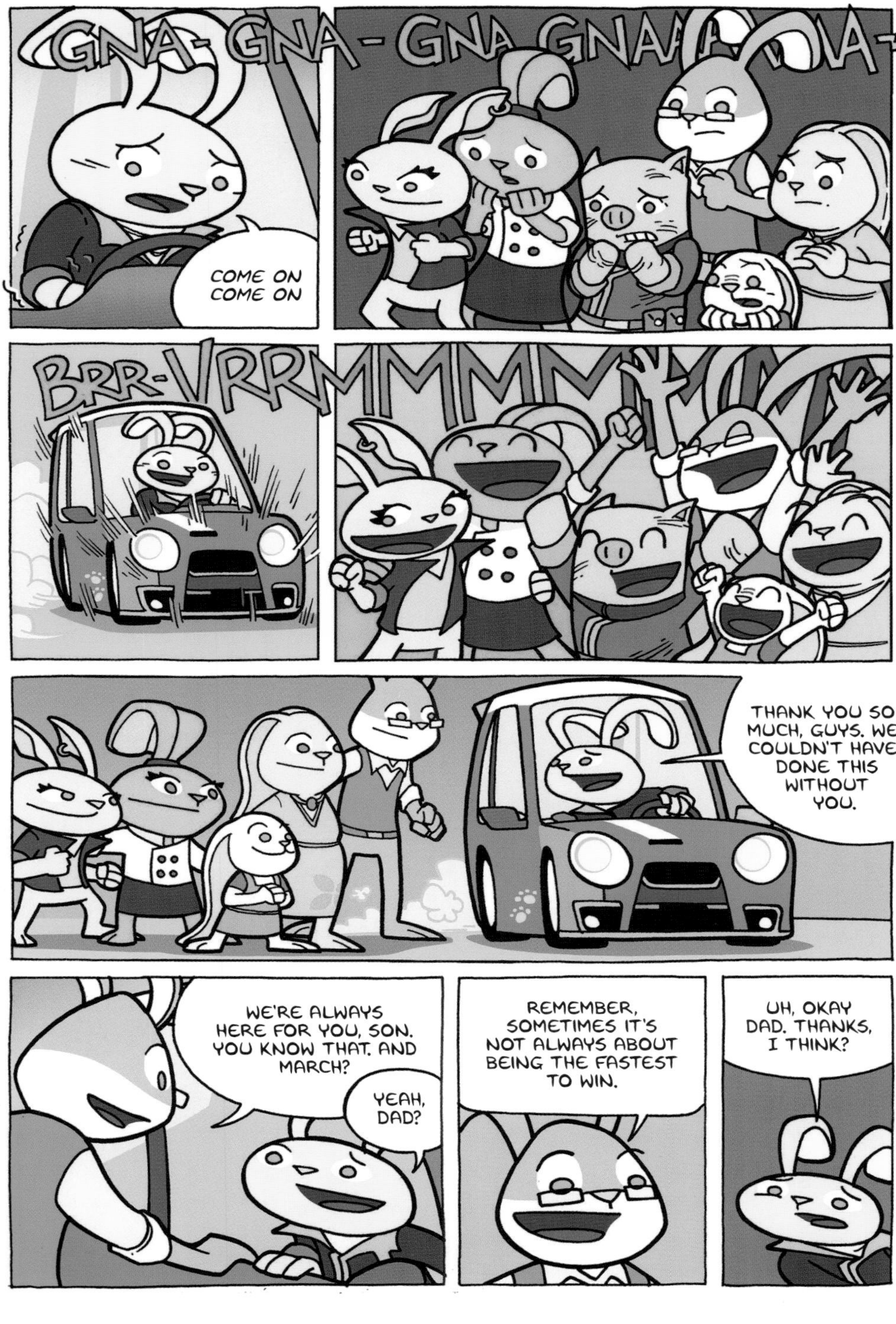
GNA-GNA-GNA GNAAAA-
COME ON COME ON
BRR-VRRMMMMM
THANK YOU SO MUCH, GUYS. WE COULDN'T HAVE DONE THIS WITHOUT YOU.
WE'RE ALWAYS HERE FOR YOU, SON. YOU KNOW THAT. AND MARCH?
YEAH, DAD?
REMEMBER, SOMETIMES IT'S NOT ALWAYS ABOUT BEING THE FASTEST TO WIN.
UH, OKAY DAD. THANKS, I THINK?

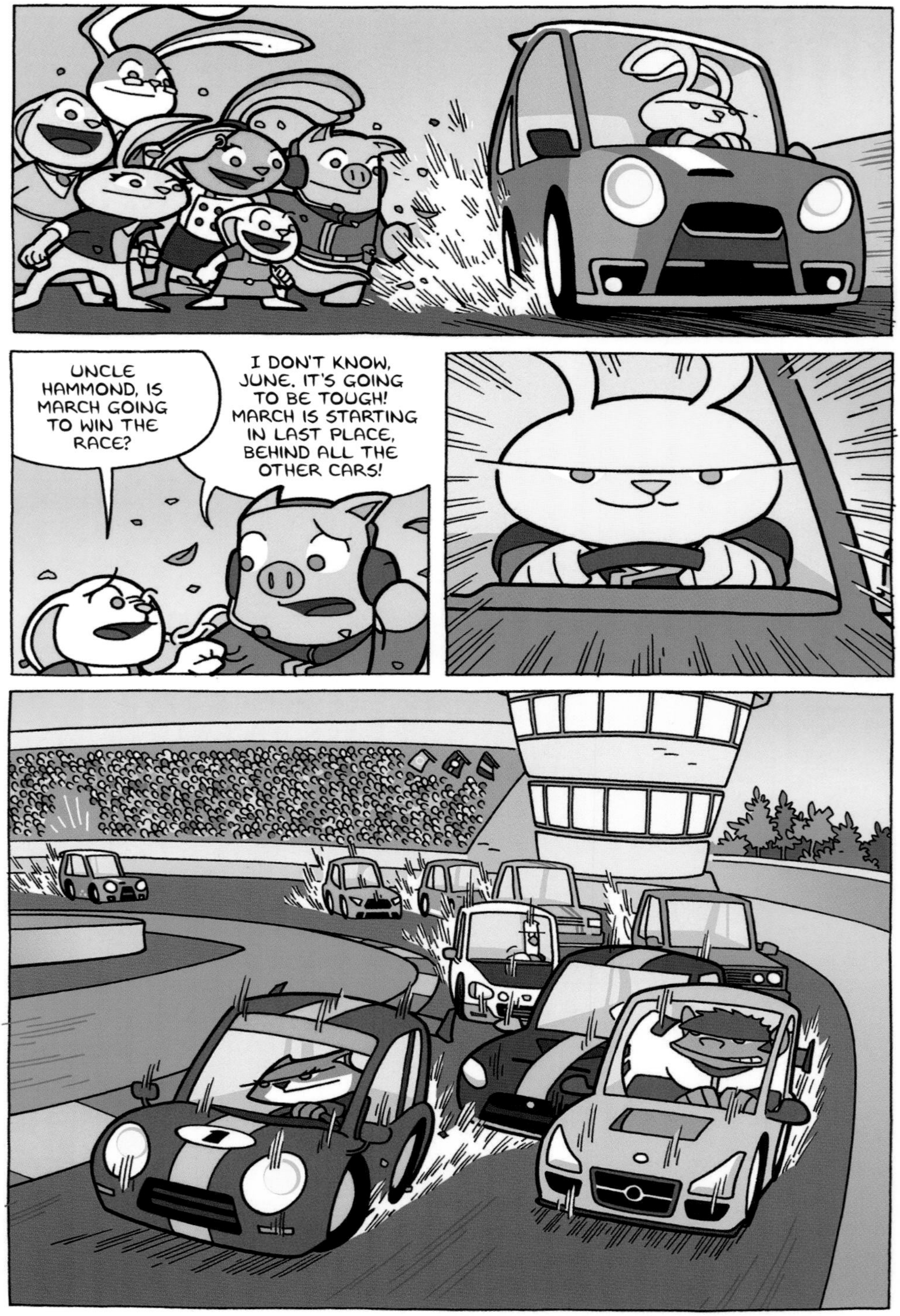
UNCLE HAMMOND, IS MARCH GOING TO WIN THE RACE?
I DON'T KNOW, JUNE. IT'S GOING TO BE TOUGH! MARCH IS STARTING IN LAST PLACE, BEHIND ALL THE OTHER CARS!

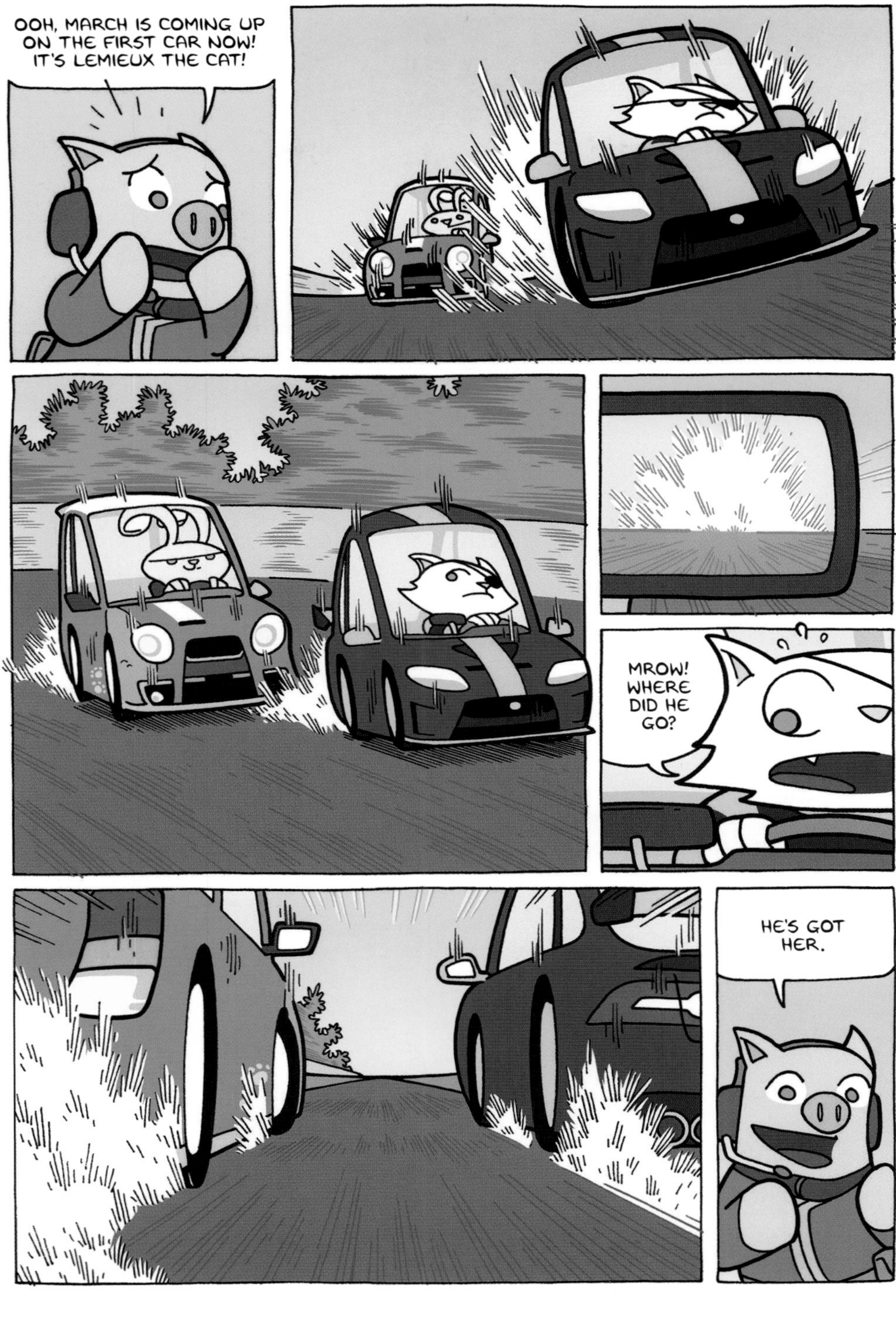
OOH, MARCH IS COMING UP ON THE FIRST CAR NOW! IT'S LEMIEUX THE CAT!
MROW! WHERE DID HE GO?
HE'S GOT HER.

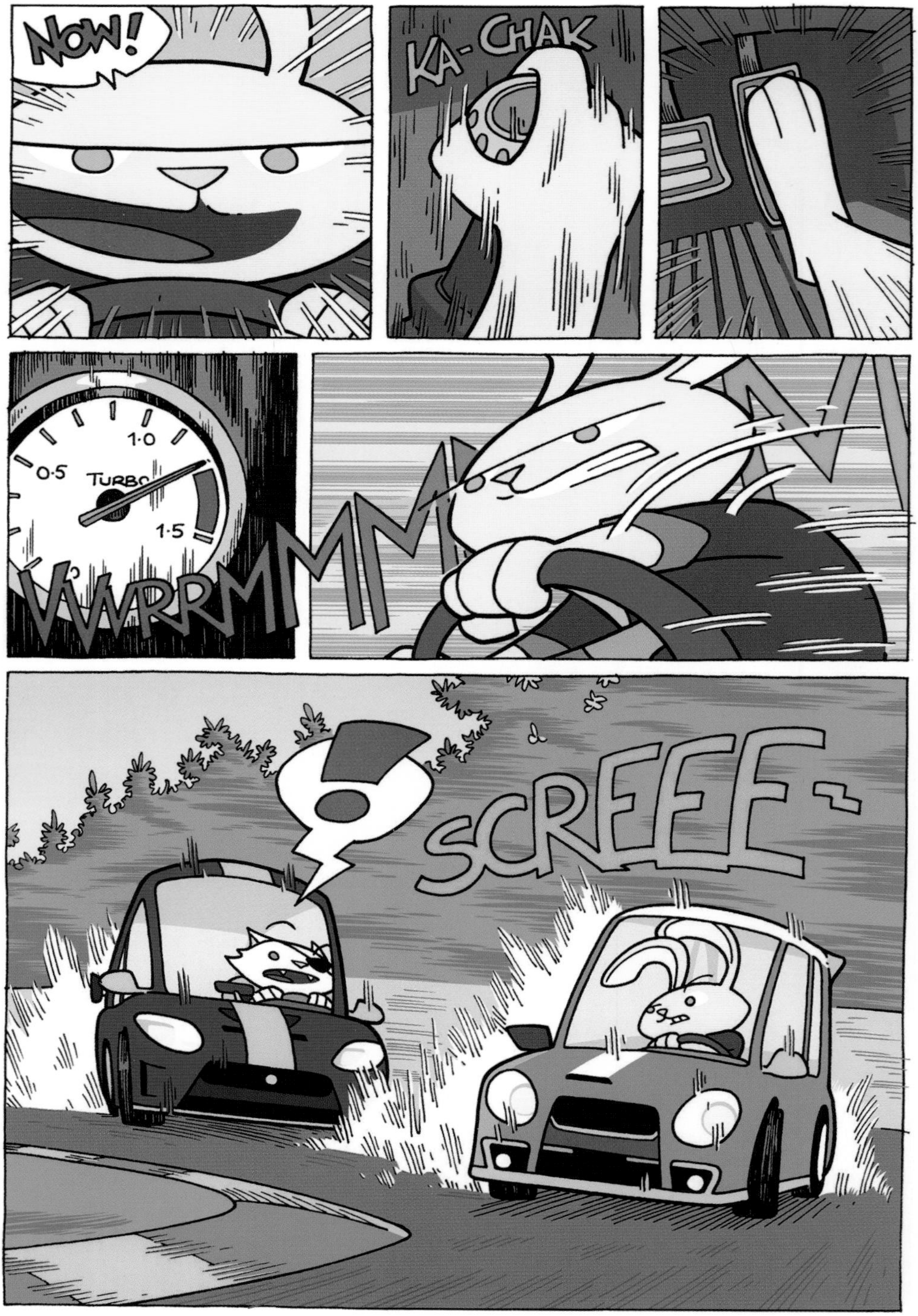
NOW!
KA-CHAK
1.0
0.5
TURBO
1.5
VVRRMMMM
SCREEE-

YEAHHH! GO MARCH! GOGOGO!

CH-CHAK

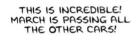

THIS IS INCREDIBLE! MARCH IS PASSING ALL THE OTHER CARS!

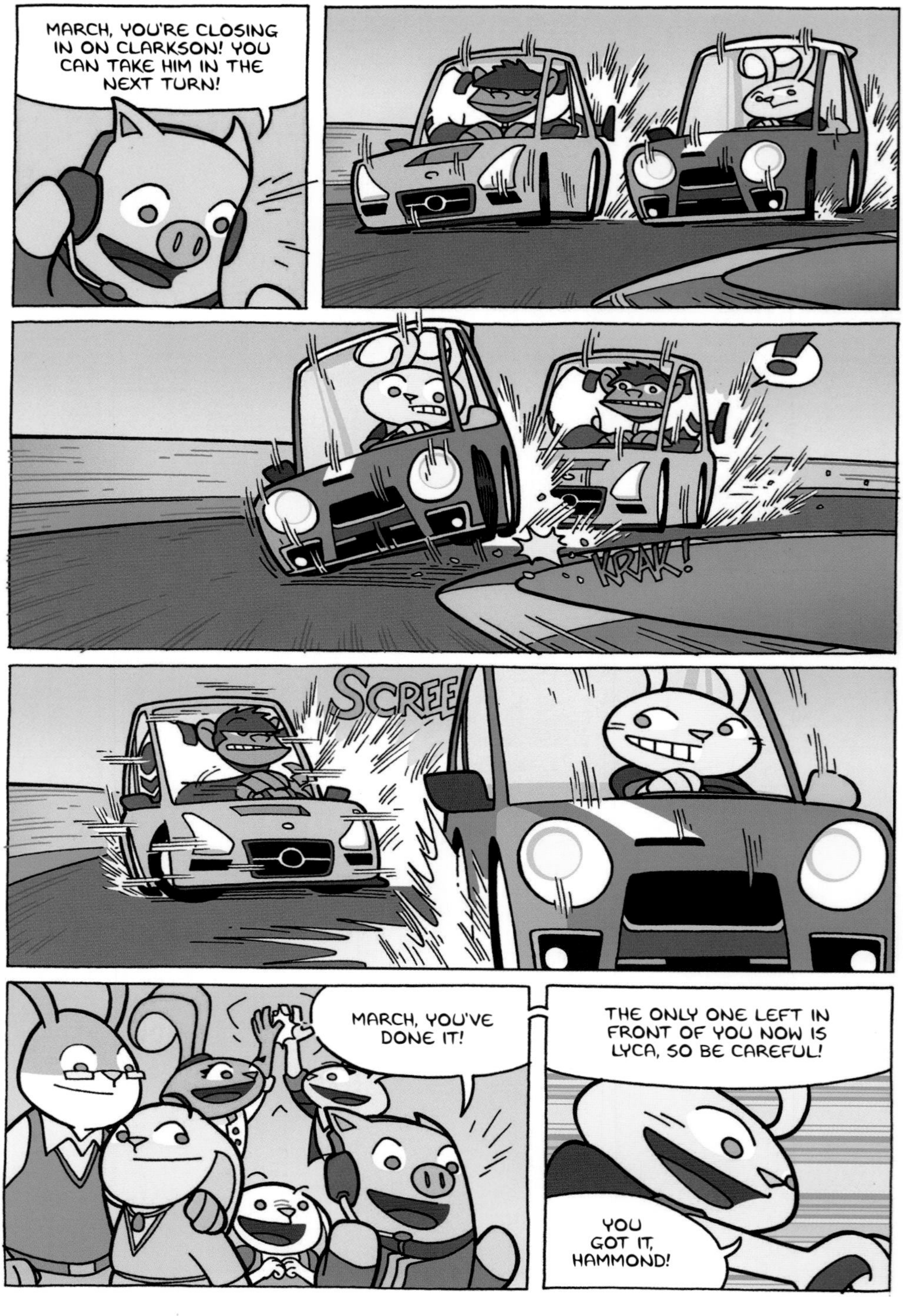
MARCH, YOU'RE CLOSING IN ON CLARKSON! YOU CAN TAKE HIM IN THE NEXT TURN!
!
KRAK!
SCREE
MARCH, YOU'VE DONE IT!
THE ONLY ONE LEFT IN FRONT OF YOU NOW IS LYCA, SO BE CAREFUL!
YOU GOT IT, HAMMOND!

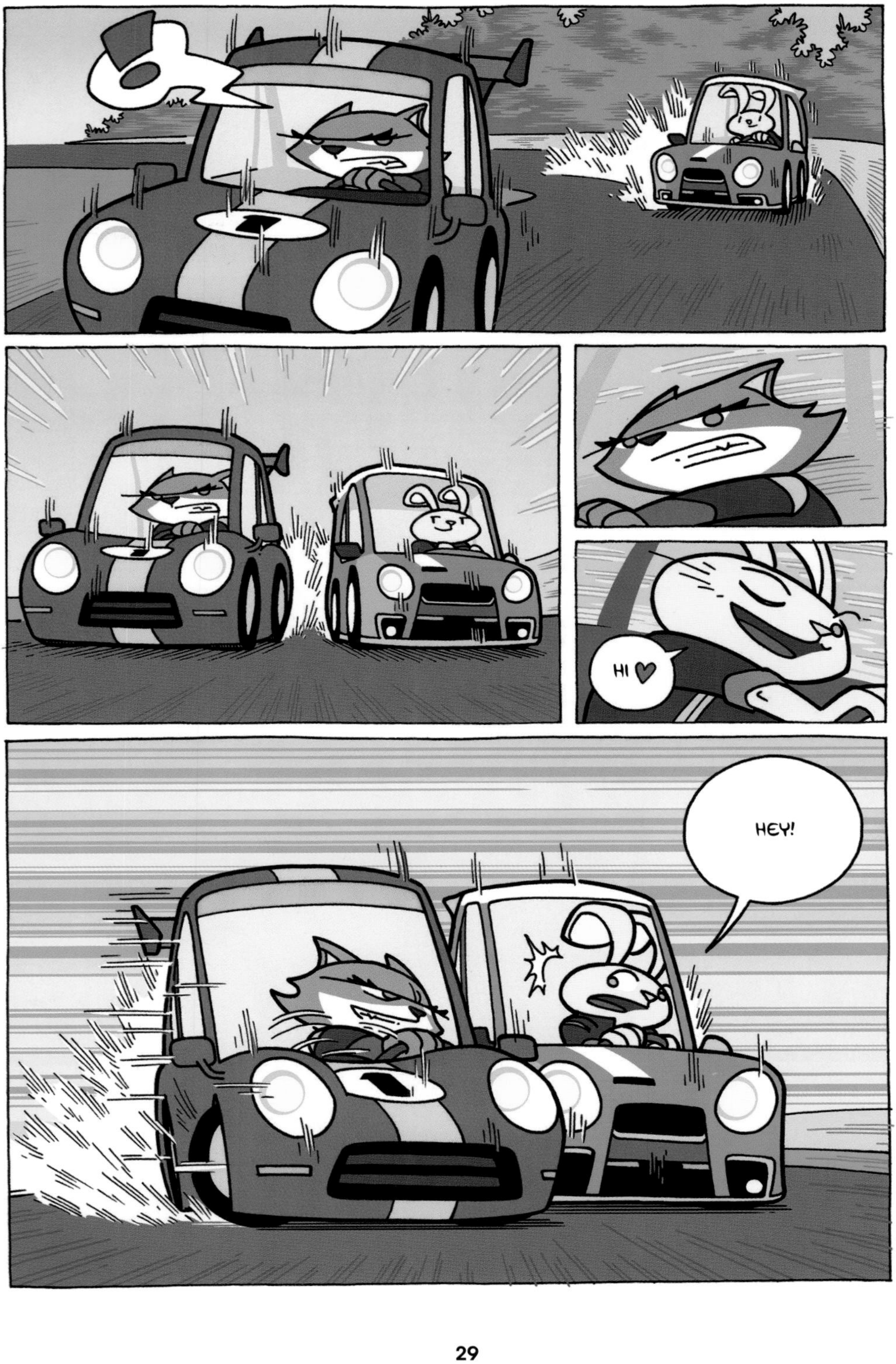
HI ♥
HEY!

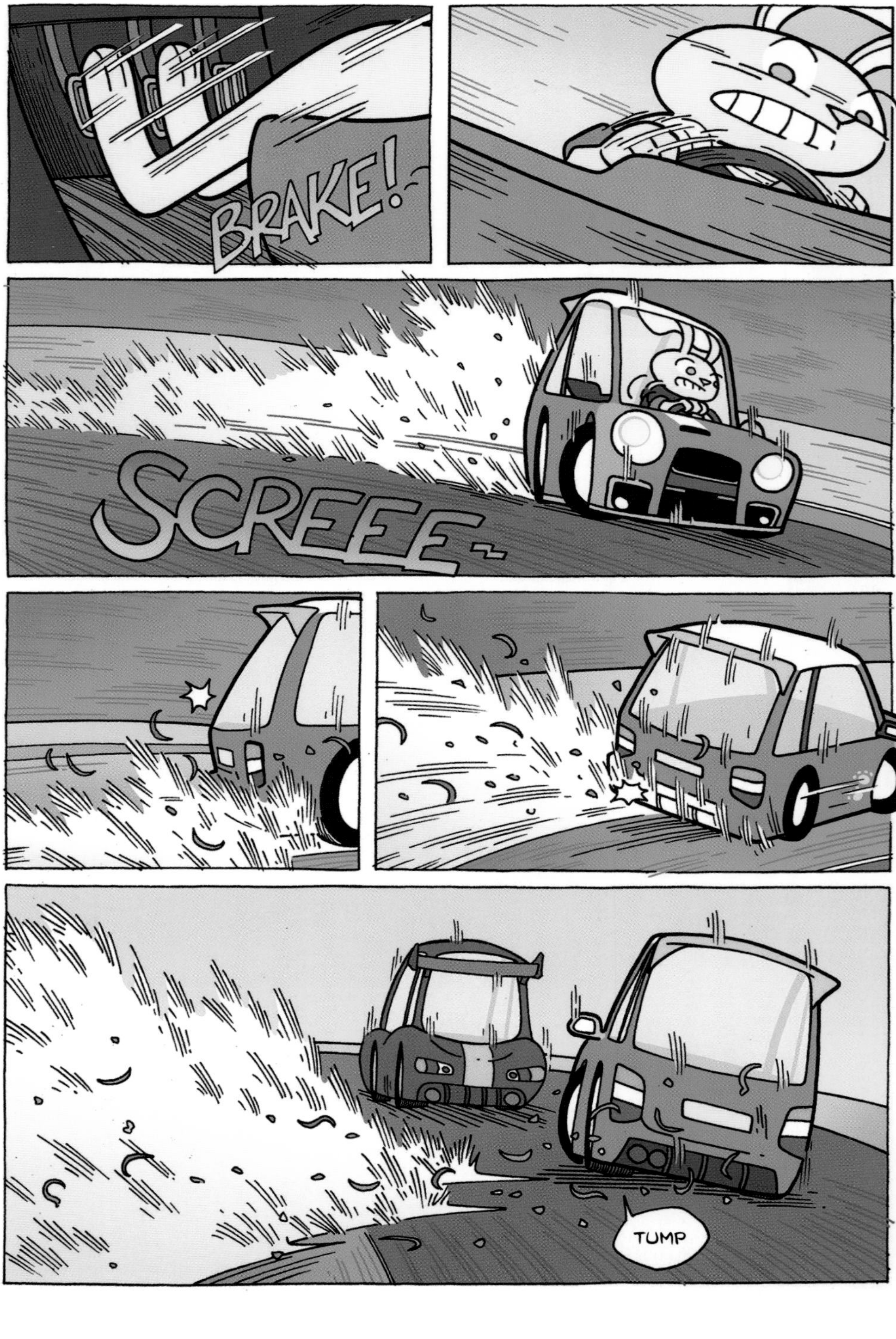
BRAKE!
SCREEE
TUMP

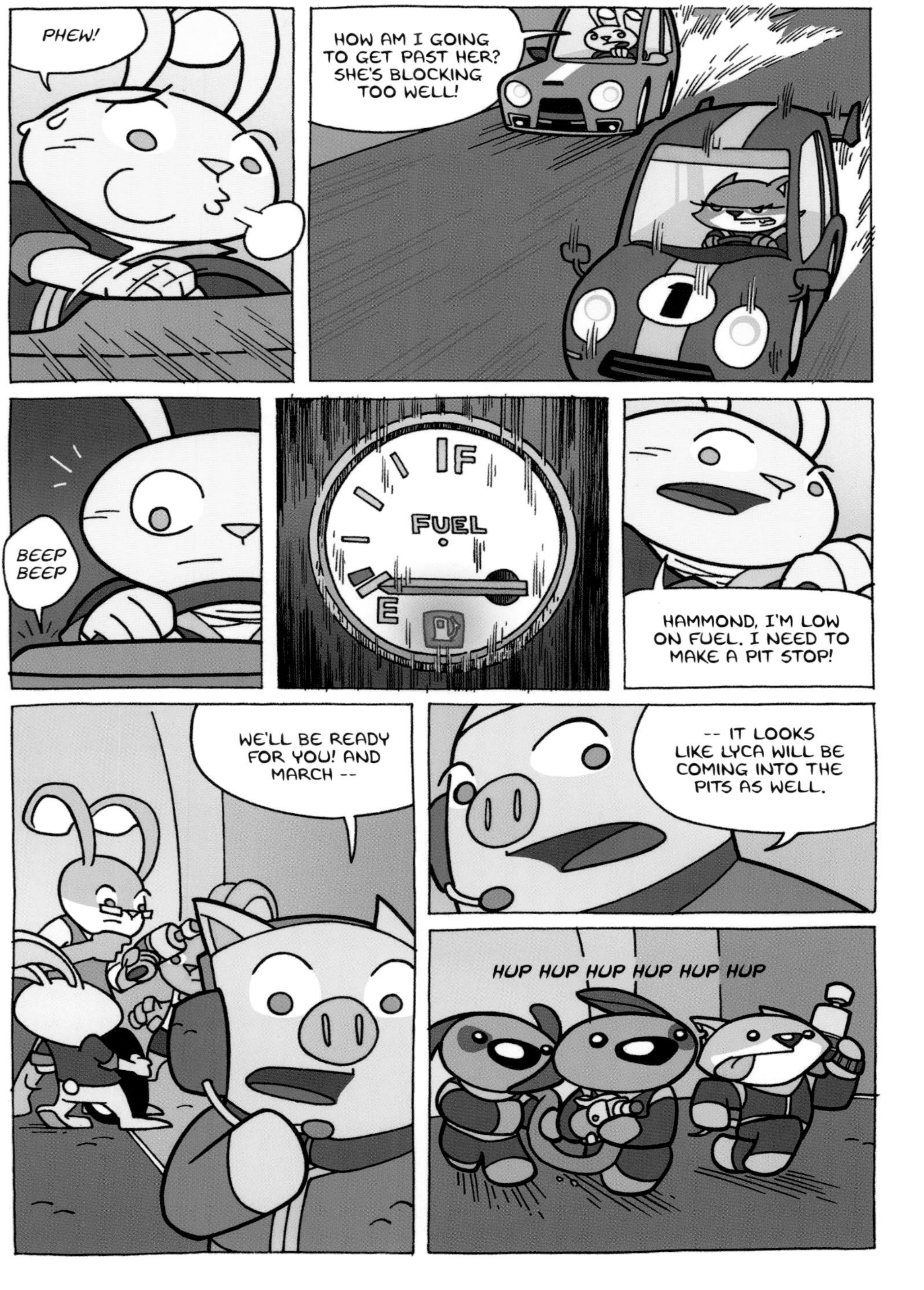
PHEW!
HOW AM I GOING TO GET PAST HER? SHE'S BLOCKING TOO WELL!
BEEP BEEP
FUEL
F
E
HAMMOND, I'M LOW ON FUEL. I NEED TO MAKE A PIT STOP!
WE'LL BE READY FOR YOU! AND MARCH --
-- IT LOOKS LIKE LYCA WILL BE COMING INTO THE PITS AS WELL.
HUP HUP HUP HUP HUP HUP

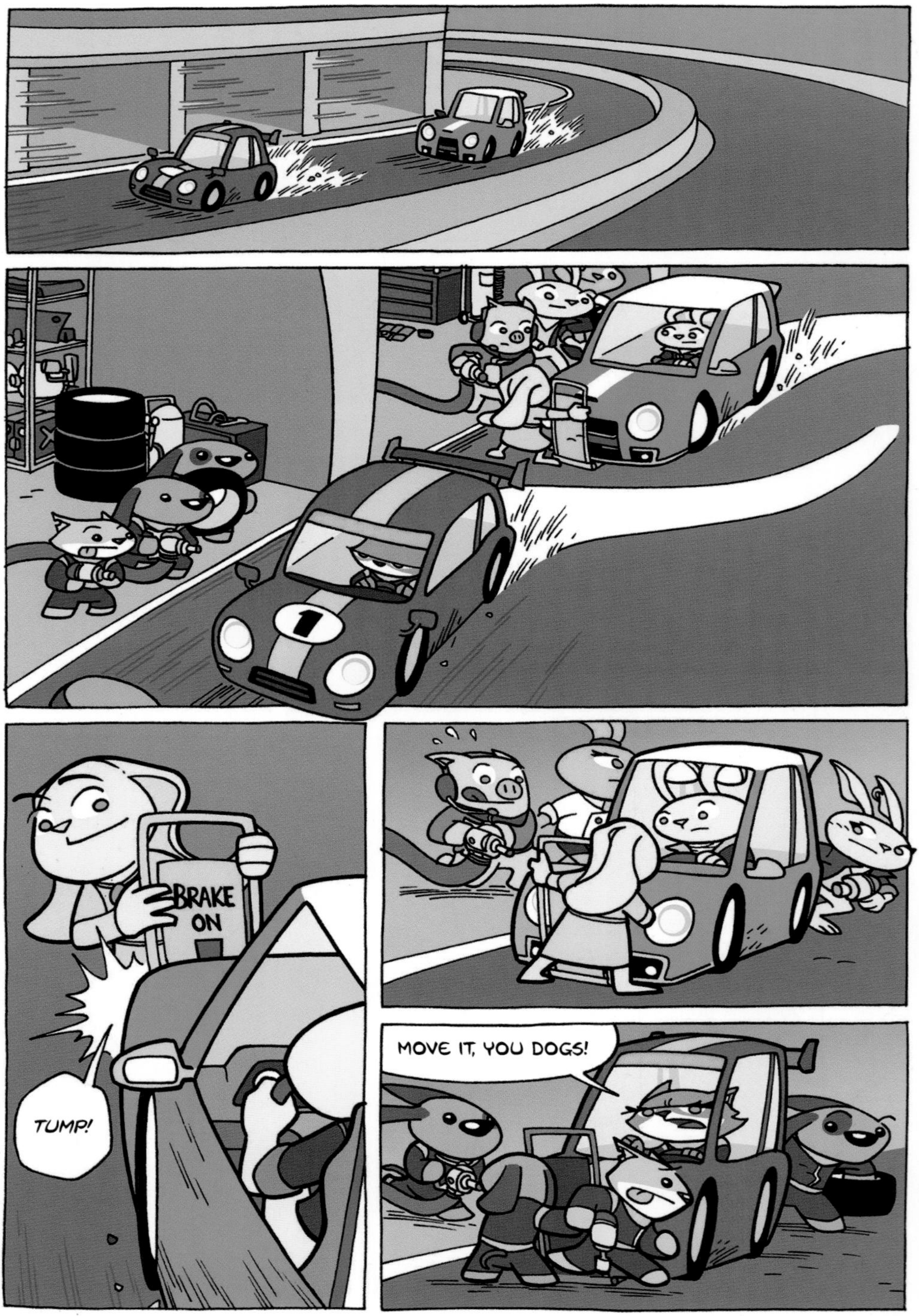
BRAKE ON
TUMP!
MOVE IT, YOU DOGS!

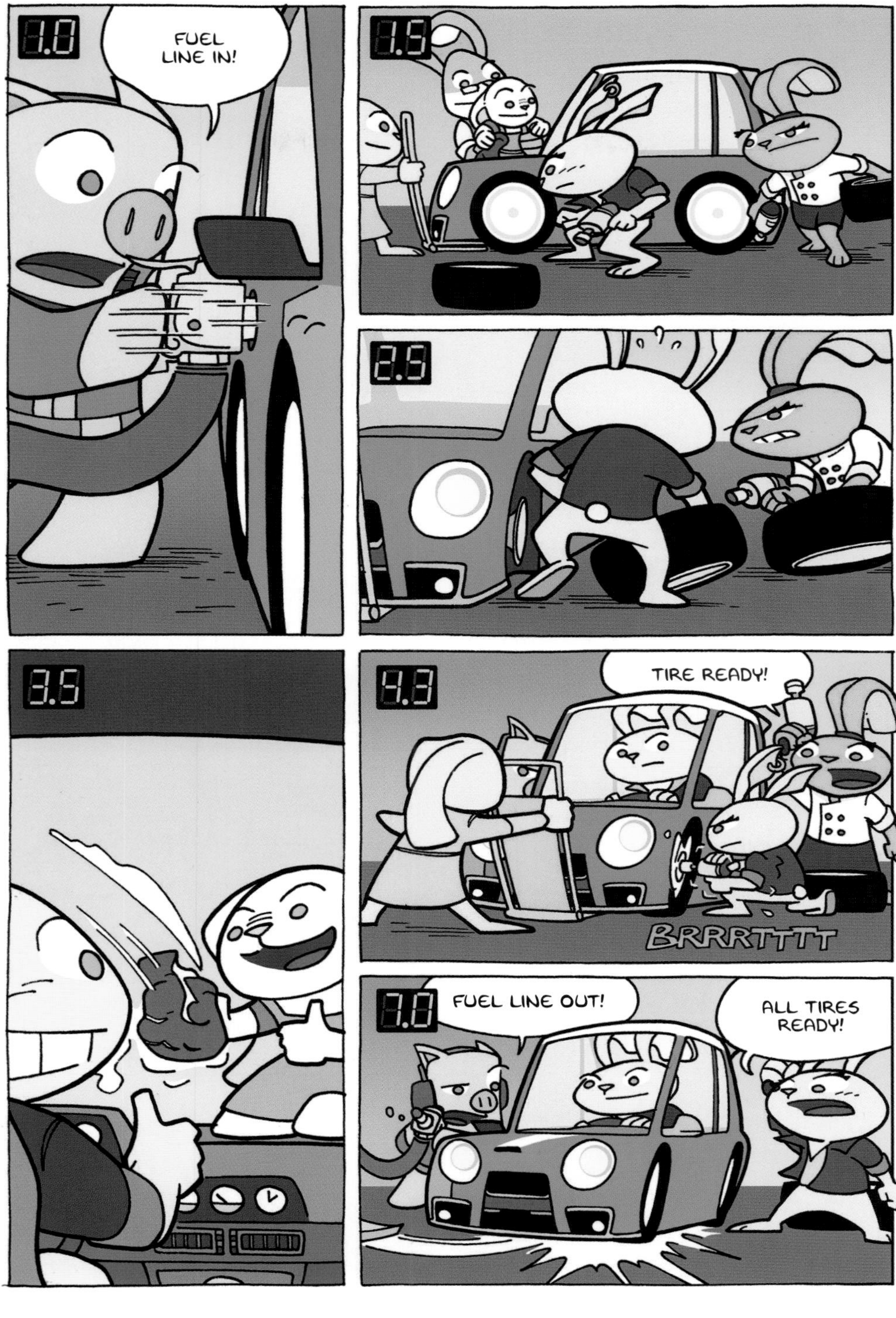
1.0
FUEL LINE IN!
1.5
2.5
3.5
4.3
TIRE READY!
BRRRTTTT
7.0
FUEL LINE OUT!
ALL TIRES READY!

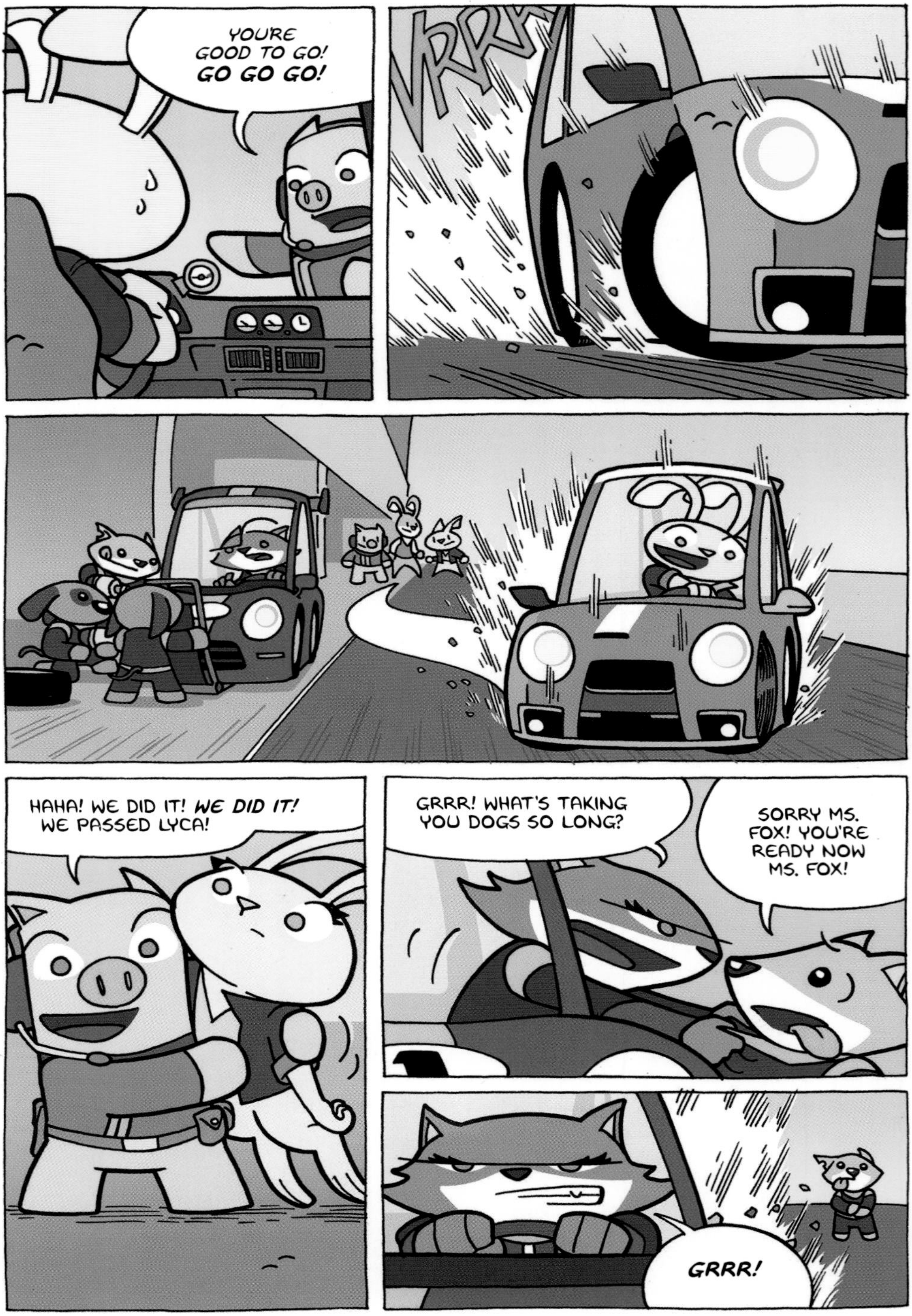
YOU'RE GOOD TO GO! GO GO GO!
VRRR
HAHA! WE DID IT! WE DID IT! WE PASSED LYCA!
GRRR! WHAT'S TAKING YOU DOGS SO LONG?
SORRY MS. FOX! YOU'RE READY NOW MS. FOX!
GRRR!

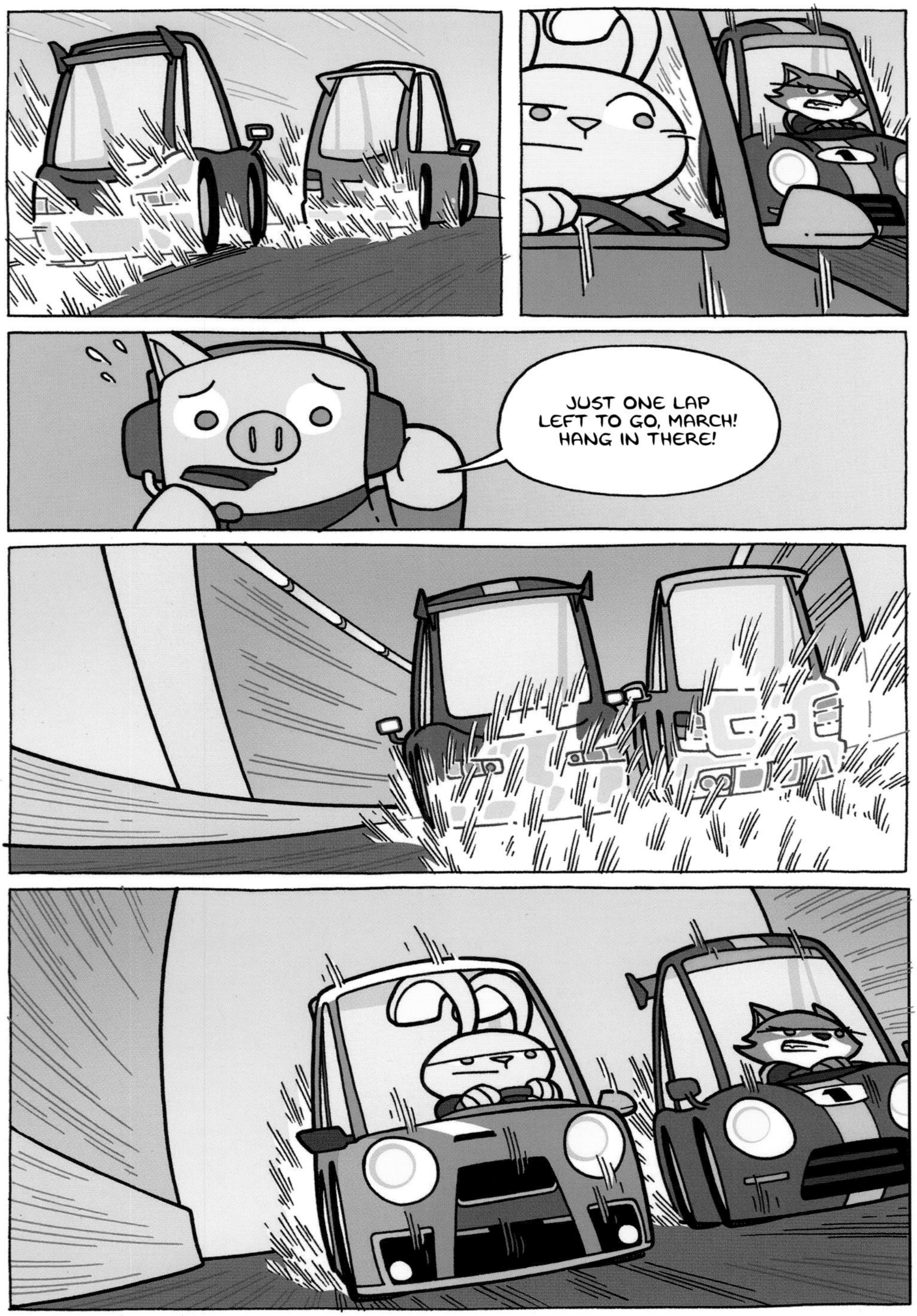
JUST ONE LAP LEFT TO GO, MARCH! HANG IN THERE!

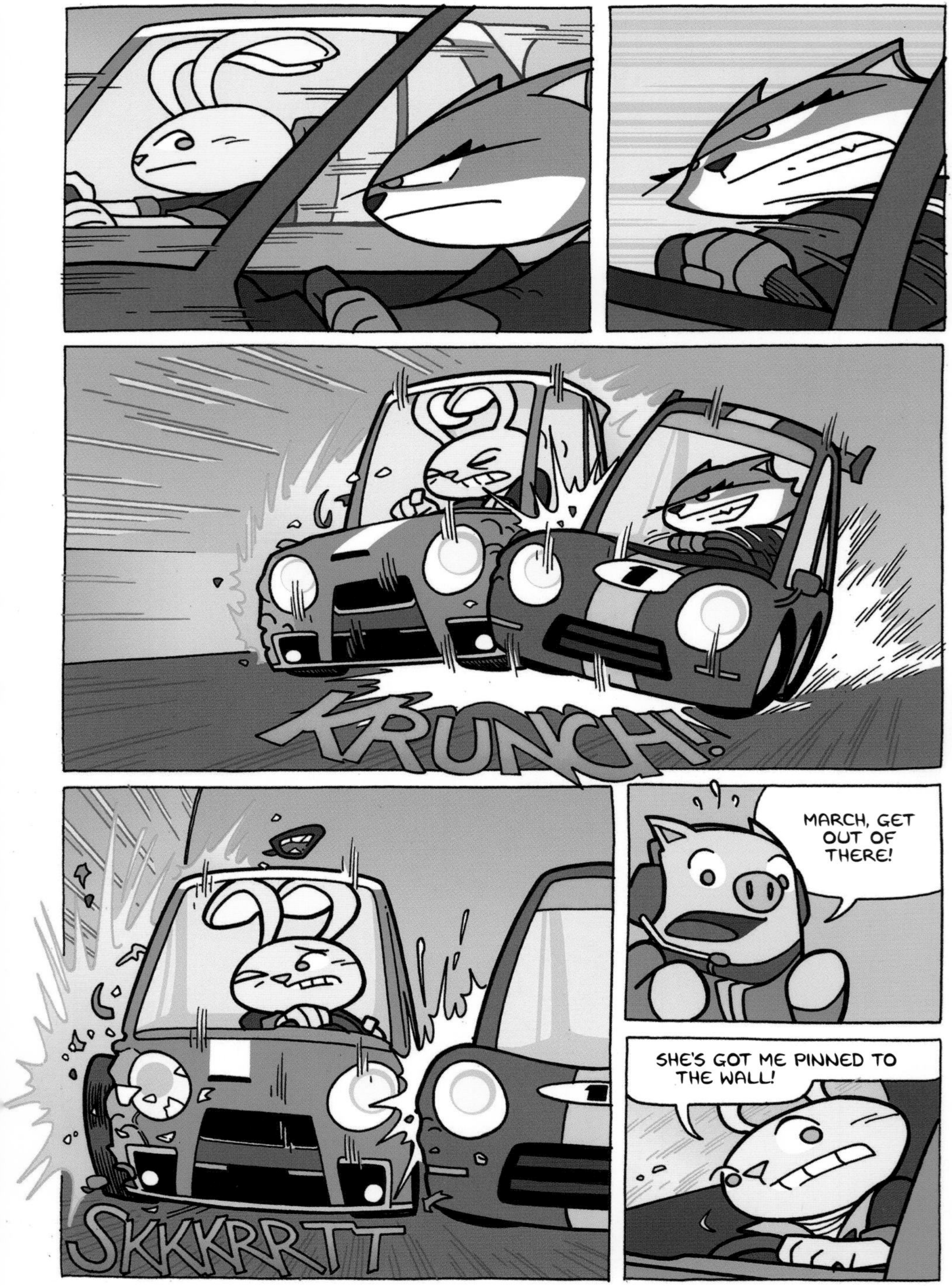
KRUNCH!
SKKKRRTT
MARCH, GET OUT OF THERE!
SHE'S GOT ME PINNED TO THE WALL!

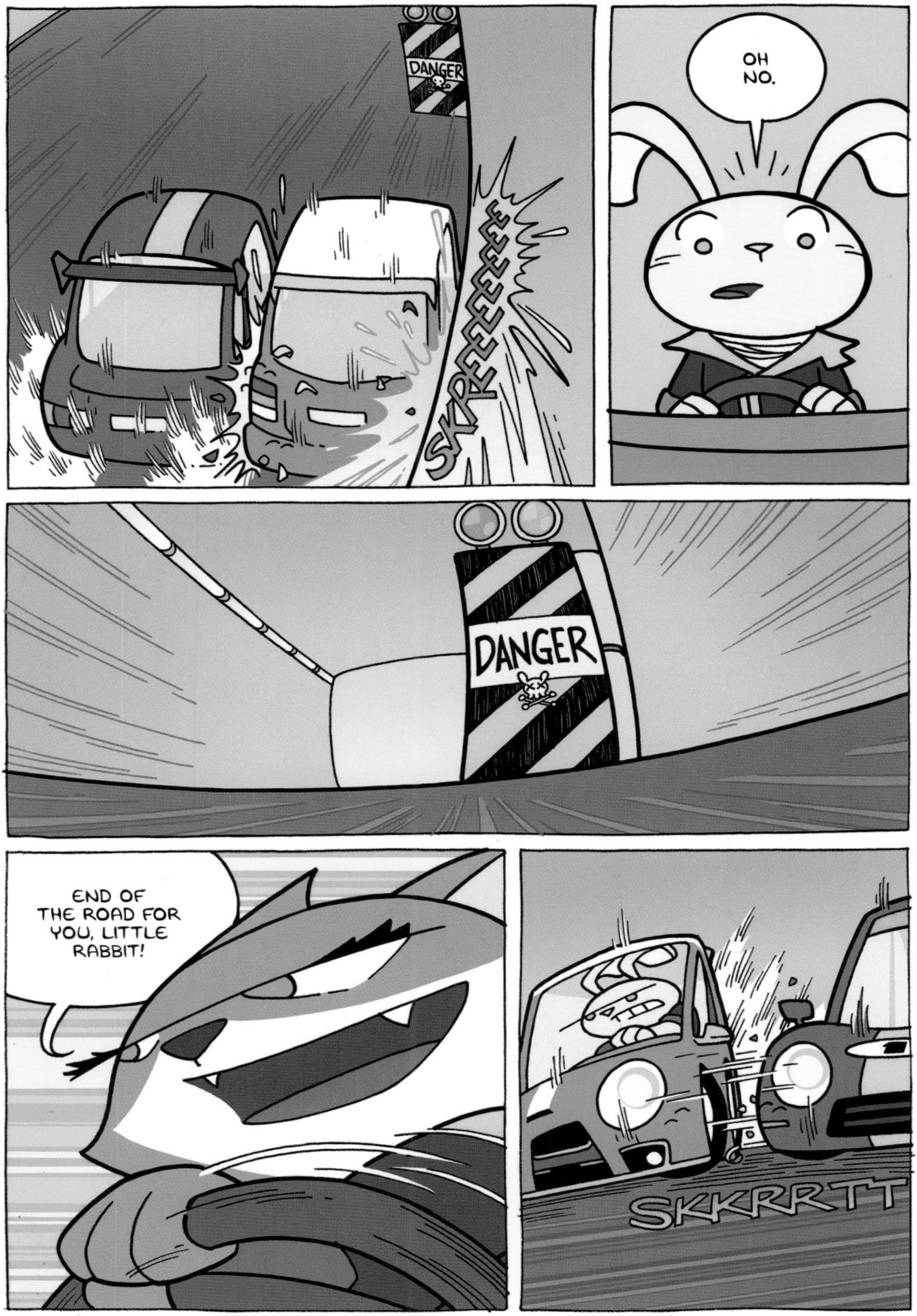
DANGER
SKREEEEEEE
OH NO.
DANGER
END OF THE ROAD FOR YOU, LITTLE RABBIT!
SKKRRTT

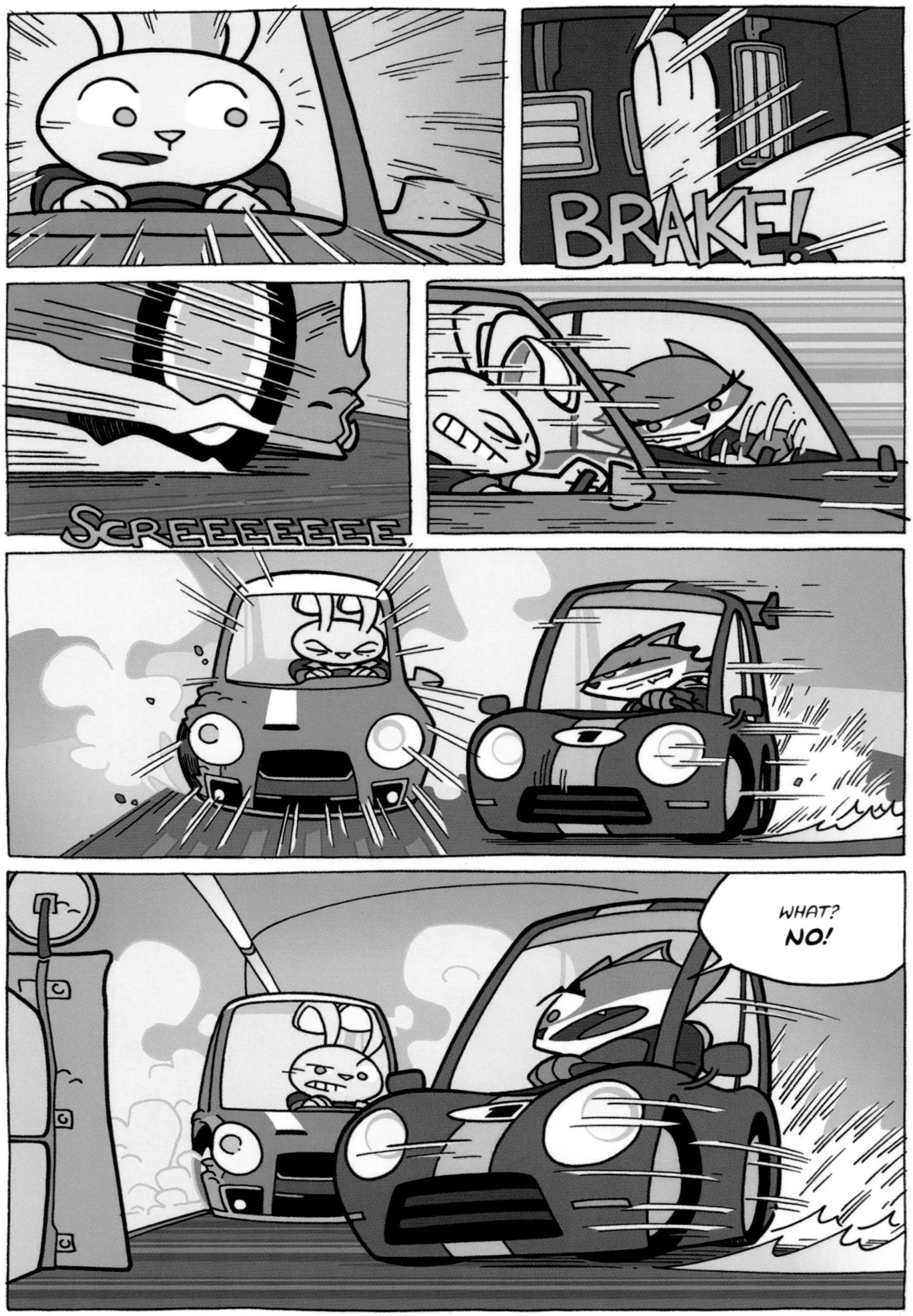
BRAKE!
SCREEEEEEEEE
WHAT?
NO!

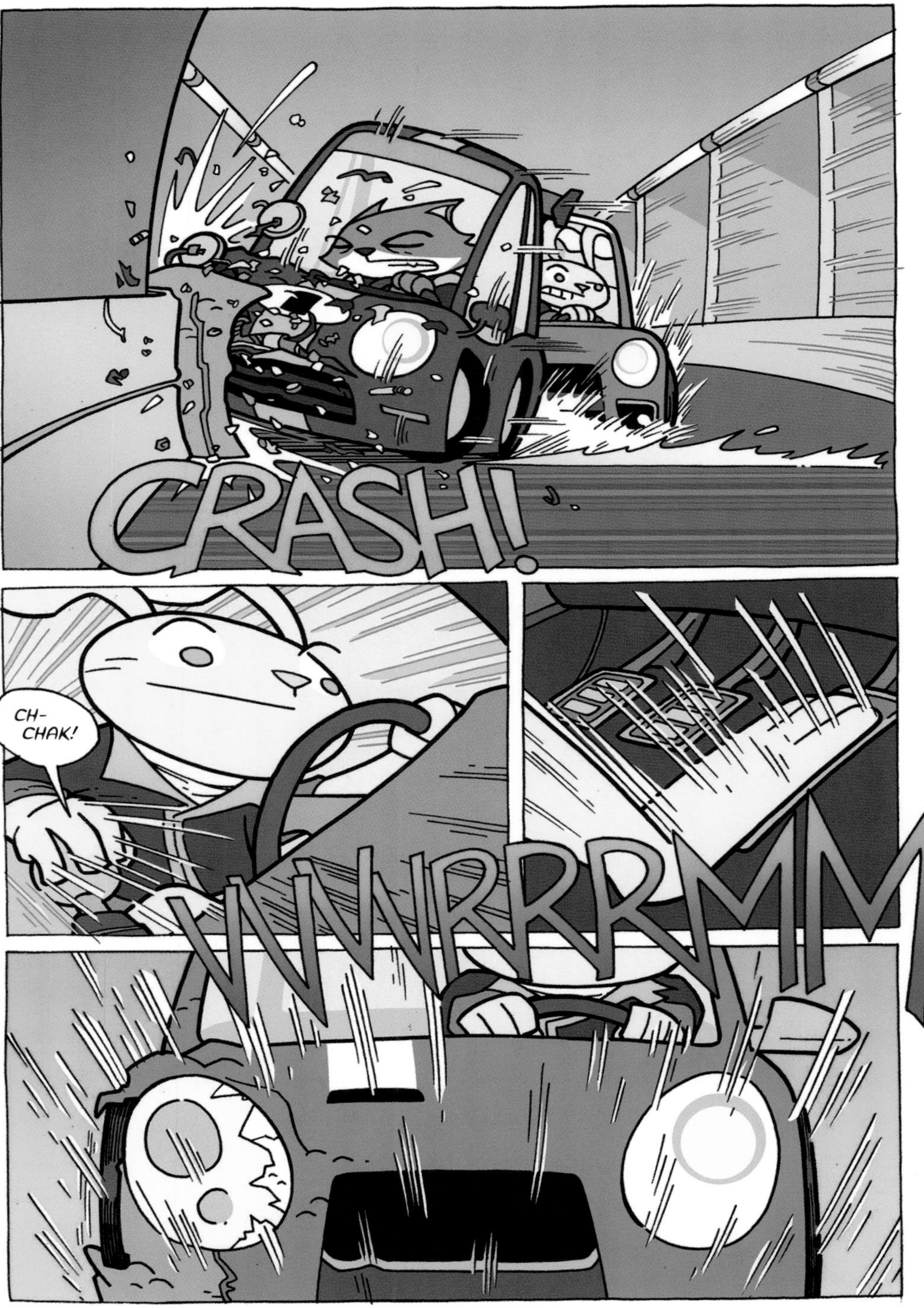
CRASH!
CH-CHAK!
VVVVRRRRMM

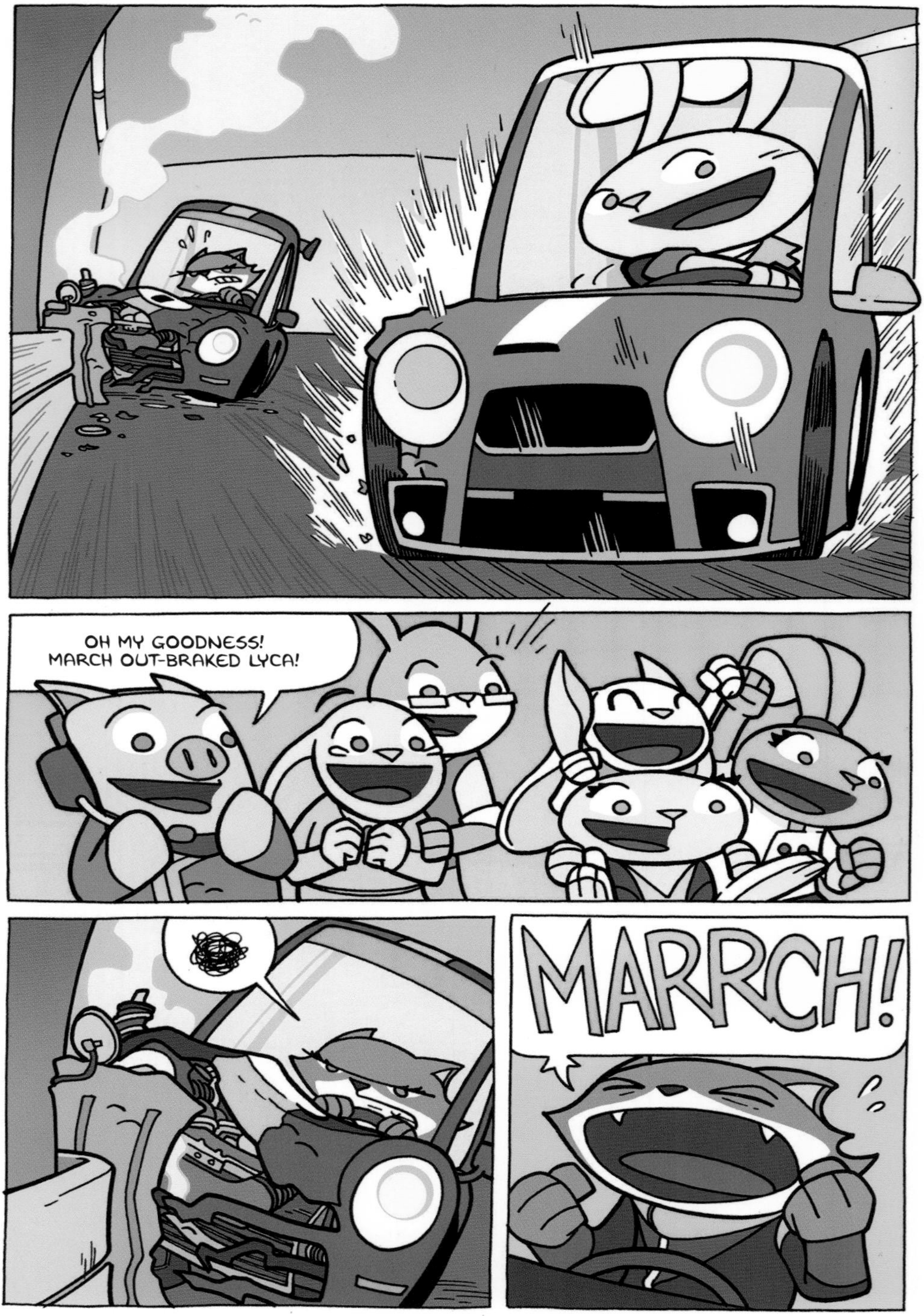
OH MY GOODNESS!
MARCH OUT-BRAKED LYCA!
MARRCH!

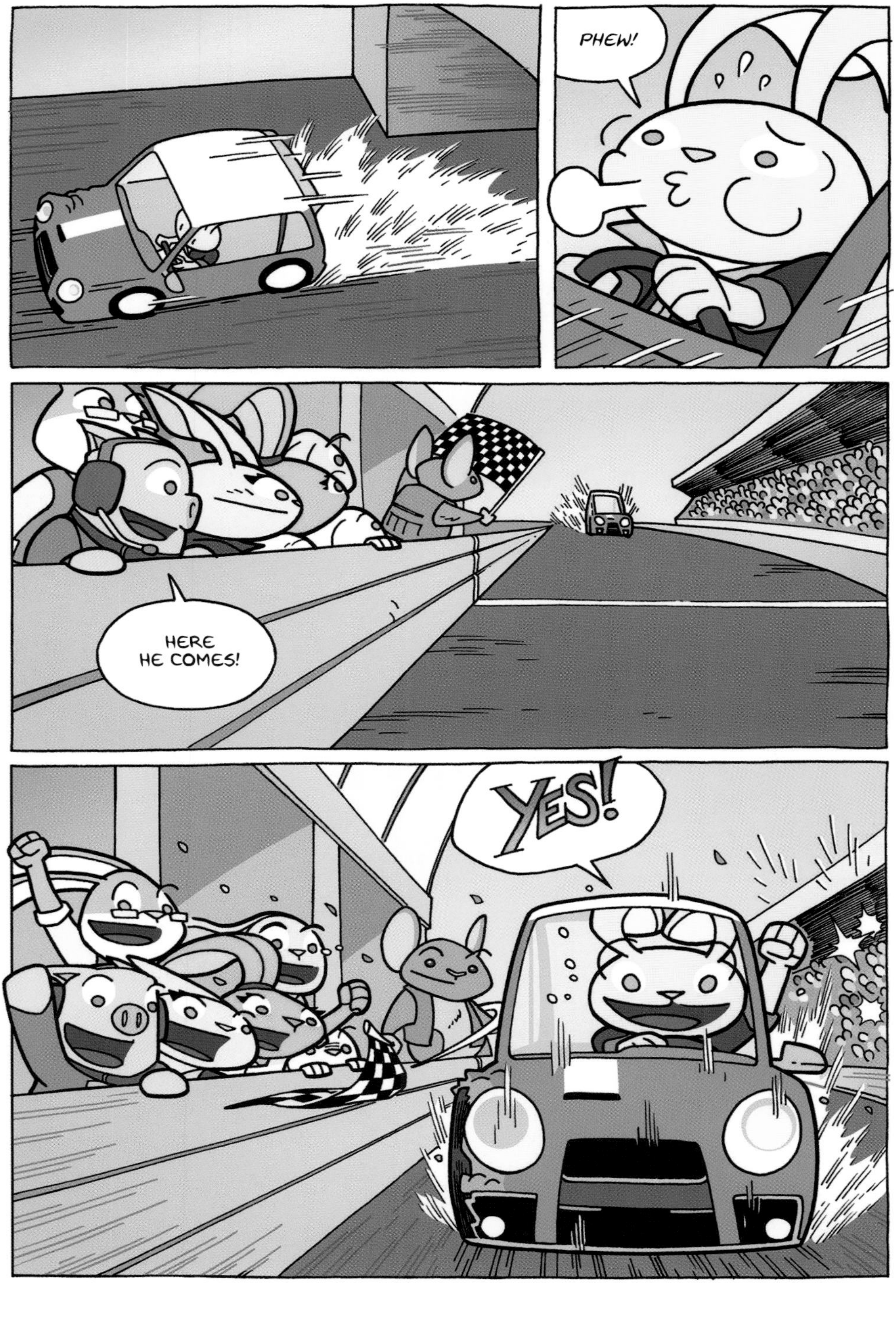
PHEW!
HERE HE COMES!
YES!

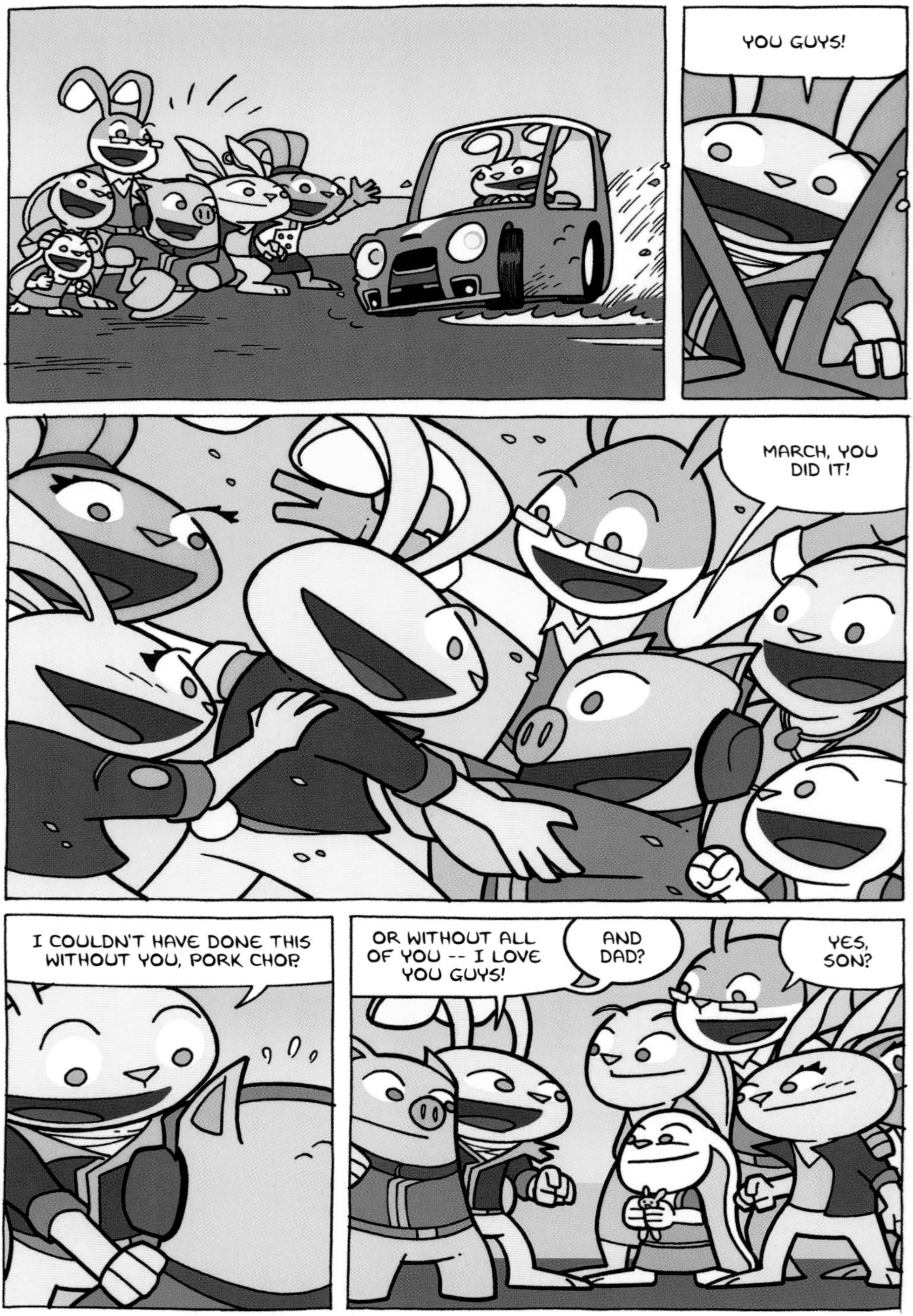
YOU GUYS!
MARCH, YOU DID IT!
I COULDN'T HAVE DONE THIS WITHOUT YOU, PORK CHOP.
OR WITHOUT ALL OF YOU -- I LOVE YOU GUYS!
AND DAD?
YES, SON?

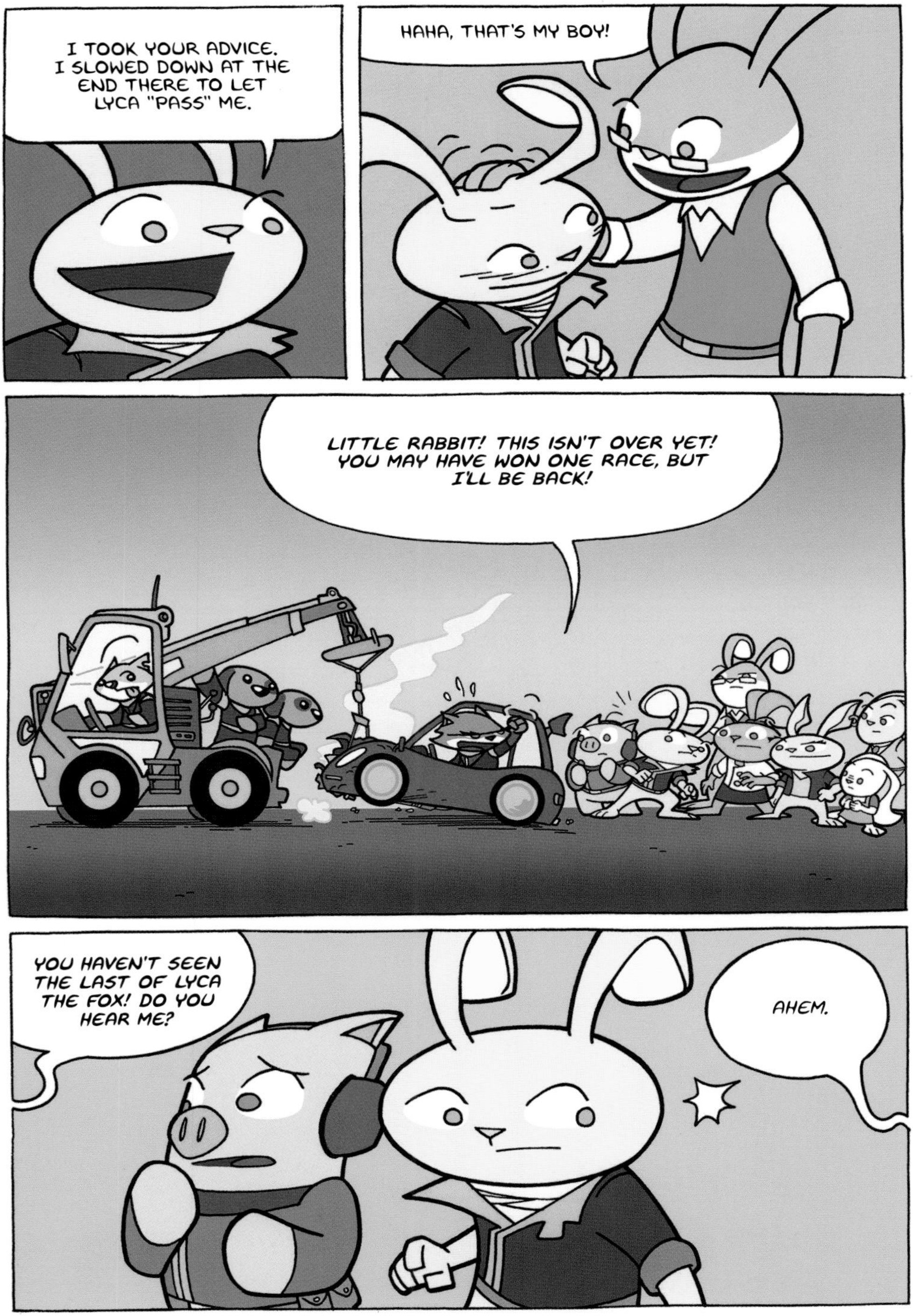
I TOOK YOUR ADVICE. I SLOWED DOWN AT THE END THERE TO LET LYCA "PASS" ME.
HAHA, THAT'S MY BOY!
LITTLE RABBIT! THIS ISN'T OVER YET! YOU MAY HAVE WON ONE RACE, BUT I'LL BE BACK!
YOU HAVEN'T SEEN THE LAST OF LYCA THE FOX! DO YOU HEAR ME?
AHEM.

ALAN TUTTLE!!

THAT'S ME.

MARCH, AS THIS YEAR'S SPECIAL GUEST OF HAREWOOD SPEEDWAY, I AM PROUD TO PRESENT YOUR PRIZE FOR FIRST PLACE, THE GOLDEN CARROT!

I ALSO HAVE A PERSONAL QUESTION I'D LIKE TO ASK YOU -- HOW WOULD YOU LIKE TO COME DRIVE FOR ME AND MY NEW RACE TEAM?

FOR REAL? I- I MEAN, YES! I WOULD BE HONORED TO!

THAT WAS A FINE BIT OF DRIVING OUT THERE, KIDDO! YOU REMINDED ME OF MYSELF WHEN I WAS A YOUNG HATCHLING!

WINK!

BUT! WE'LL HAVE PLENTY OF TIME TO TALK TOMORROW. FOR NOW, JUST ENJOY YOUR VICTORY!

THANK YOU MR. TUTTLE, BUT THIS ISN'T MY VICTORY.

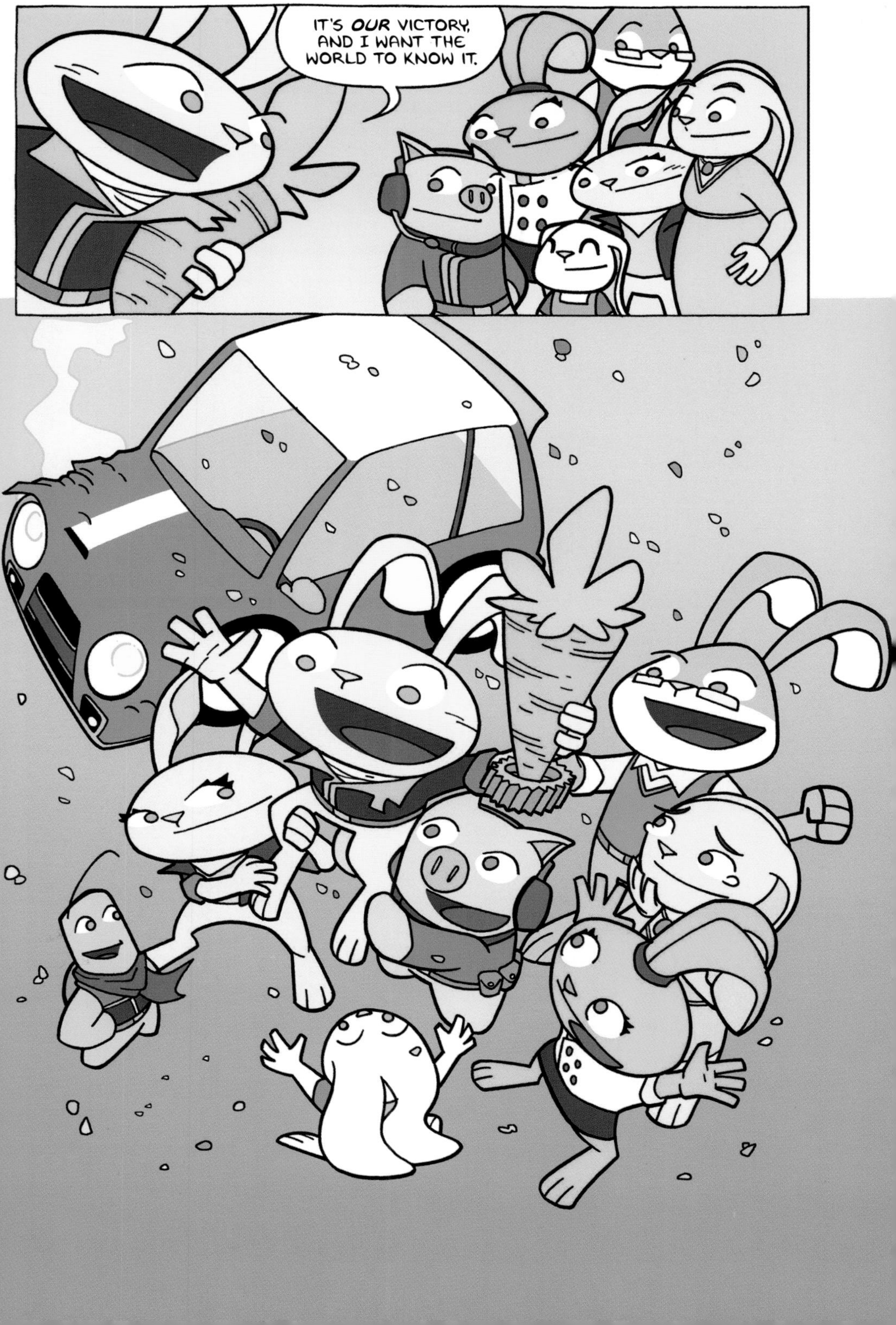
IT'S OUR VICTORY, AND I WANT THE WORLD TO KNOW IT.

SKETCHES

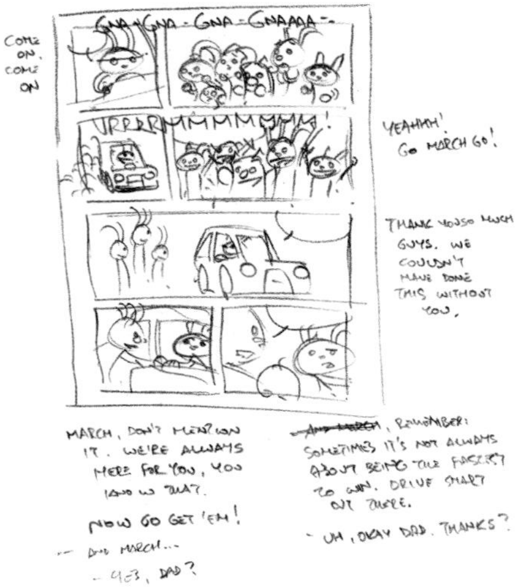
GNA-GNA-GNA-GNAAAA-
COME ON, COME ON
YEAHHH! GO MARCH GO!
THANK YOU SO MUCH GUYS. WE COULDN'T HAVE DONE THIS WITHOUT YOU.
NOW GO GET 'EM!
UH, OKAY DAD. THANKS?

1. Thumbnail roughs

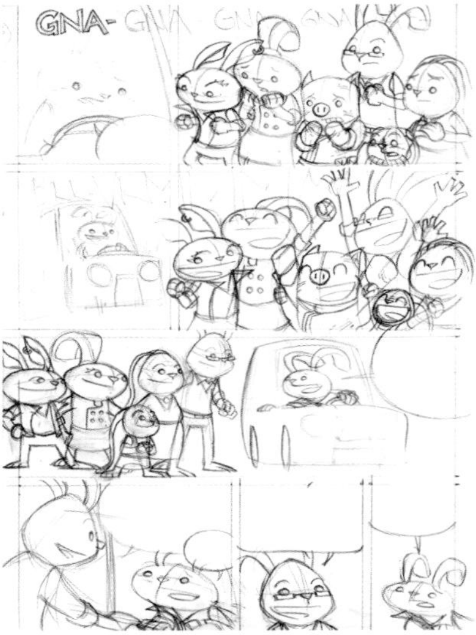
GNA-

2. Pencils

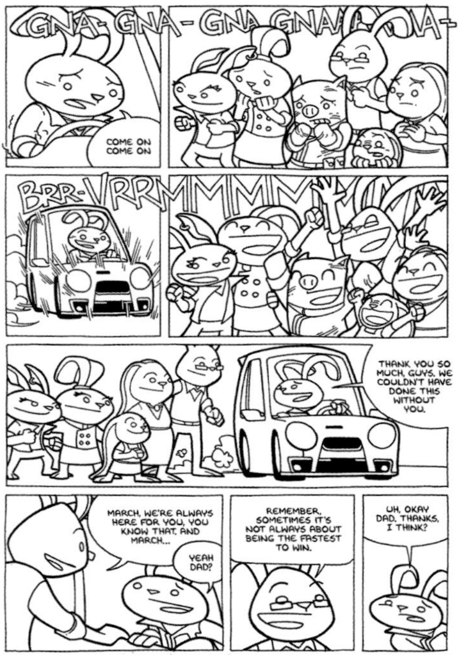
COME ON
COME ON
BRR-VRRMMMMM
THANK YOU SO MUCH, GUYS. WE COULDN'T HAVE DONE THIS WITHOUT YOU.
MARCH, WE'RE ALWAYS HERE FOR YOU, YOU KNOW THAT. AND MARCH...
YEAH DAD?
REMEMBER, SOMETIMES IT'S NOT ALWAYS ABOUT BEING THE FASTEST TO WIN.
UH, OKAY DAD. THANKS, I THINK?

3. Inks & digital lettering

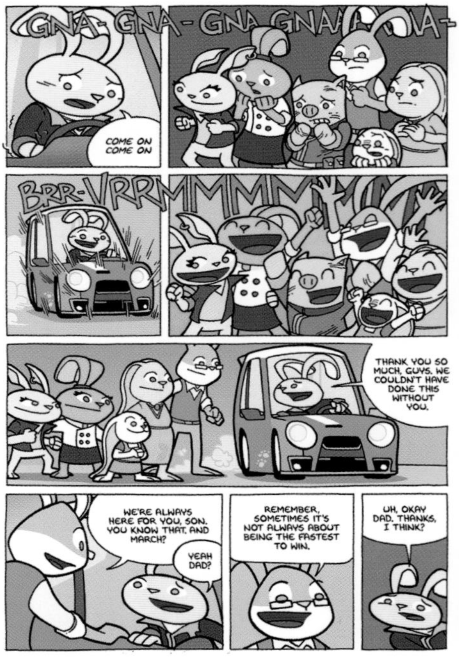
COME ON
COME ON
BRR-VRRMMMMM
THANK YOU SO MUCH, GUYS. WE COULDN'T HAVE DONE THIS WITHOUT YOU.
WE'RE ALWAYS HERE FOR YOU, SON. YOU KNOW THAT. AND MARCH?
YEAH DAD?
REMEMBER, SOMETIMES IT'S NOT ALWAYS ABOUT BEING THE FASTEST TO WIN.
UH, OKAY DAD. THANKS, I THINK?

4. Final colors

Character design sketches

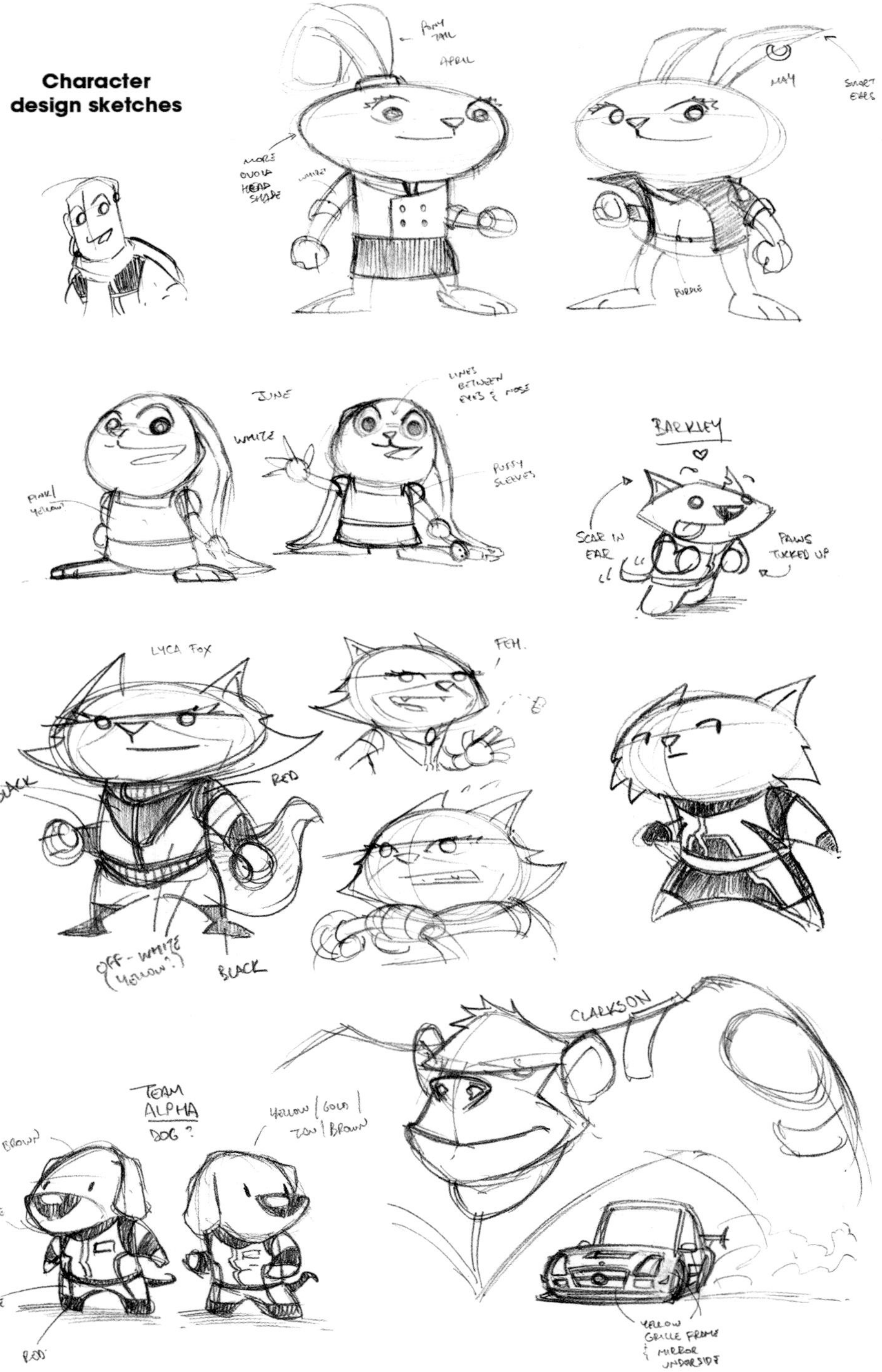
PONY TAIL
APRIL
MORE OVOID HEAD SHAPE
WHITE
MAY
SHORT EARS
PURPLE
JUNE
LINES BETWEEN EYES & NOSE
WHITE
PUFFY SLEEVES
PINK/ YELLOW
BARKLEY
SCAR IN EAR
PAWS TUCKED UP
LYCA FOX
FEH.
BLACK
RED
OFF-WHITE (YELLOW?)
BLACK
CLARKSON
TEAM ALPHA DOG?
YELLOW / GOLD / TAN / BROWN
BROWN
WHITE
WHITE
RED
YELLOW GRILLE FRAME & MIRROR UNDERSIDE

KEAN SOO

Kean Soo was born in the United Kingdom, grew up in various parts of Canada and Hong Kong, trained as an electrical engineer, and now draws comics for a living. A former assistant editor and contributor for the FLIGHT comics anthology, Kean also created the award-winning Jellaby series of graphic novels.

Kean's first car was a 1991 Volkswagen GTI 16V, which he drove and (very occasionally) raced for over 10 years.

Kean would also like to thank Judy Hansen, Donnie Lemke, Brann Garvey, Tony Cliff, Kazu Kibuishi, everyone in the FLIGHT crew, and Tory Woollcott for making March Grand Prix such a joy to work on.